Playback

Playback
Carla Malden

RARE BIRD
LOS ANGELES, CALIF.

RARE BIRD

THIS IS A GENUINE RARE BIRD BOOK

Rare Bird Books
6044 North Figueroa Street
Los Angeles, California 90042
rarebirdbooks.com

Copyright © 2025 by Carla Malden

FIRST HARDCOVER EDITION

Rare Bird Books supports copyright. Copyright fuels creativity, encourages diverse voices, promotes free speech, and creates a vibrant culture. Thank you for buying an authorized edition of this book and for complying with copyright laws by not reproducing, scanning, or distributing any part of it in any form without permission. You are supporting writers and allowing Rare Bird Books to continue to publish books for readers to enjoy and appreciate.

All rights reserved, including the right to reproduce this book
or portions thereof in any form whatsoever, including
but not limited to print, audio, and electronic.

For more information, address:
Rare Bird Books Subsidiary Rights Department
6044 North Figueroa Street
Los Angeles, California 90042

Set in Adobe Garamond
Printed in the United States

10 9 8 7 6 5 4 3 2 1

Library of Congress Cataloging-in-Publication Data available upon request

*For Lenny and Jasper
my hope for the future*

"...for time is the longest distance between two places."

Tennessee Williams
The Glass Menagerie

CHAPTER ONE

"Once upon a time there was a summer."

I pull the covers close under Joni's chin and stretch out next to her, propping my head against the plush unicorn pillow that guards her bed. Even though I'm on top of the covers and she's underneath, I can't help but lean into the warmth of her little body snuggled in, fighting sleep.

"Go on," she says. "That's my favorite."

"Mine too." My chin rests on top of her head, her hair corn-silk soft. "It was a special summer."

"In San Franfrisco." Joni looks up at me, eyes preternaturally wide: *I'm not tired, I'm not tired.*

"Yes, in San Francisco."

"When you walked down the street..." Joni prompts.

"When you walked down the street, it was like being at a carnival. Everyone wore bright colors..."

"Tie-dye like my T-shirt."

"Exactly like your T-shirt. In fact, there was a girl wearing a tie-dye T-shirt just like the one you have. Her name was..."

"Joni."

Joni is the star of all the best bedtime stories.

"And one day she was walking down the street..."

"Twirling."

"That's right. How silly of me. Joni never walked. She twirled everywhere she went. So she was twirling down Ashbury Street."

"I've been there."

"Yes, you have. And a boy came up to her and handed her a flower. It was a daisy. And she kept twirling down the street… twirling…twirling…"

"Because she liked to dance. Like me."

"She loved to dance. And every time she turned around…spun around, that is…there was someone else handing her a flower. She began weaving all the flowers together—she was so good at crafty things like that—and before you know it, she had made a beautiful crown. You know what she did with that crown? She put it on top of her head! And it fit perfectly."

"She looked like the princess of flowers."

"She *was* the princess of flowers."

"Then the music…"

"Who's telling this story?" I say, poking fun. The truth is we both are. "But you're exactly right. Joni, Princess of Flowers, heard music coming from way down the street. It sounded like a flute, but no—she realized it was a recorder."

"Like we're learning to play at school."

"Exactly." I reach over and stroke the space between her eyebrows with my index finger. A downward motion—down, down, down, coaxing her into sleep. "She also heard the sound of drums and a guitar…" I continue, "…of tambourines and tinkling bells."

She laughs right on cue. Because she's four-and-three-quarters. Bells that go tinkle—so funny. But there's no swapping in another word. This is the story I tell. And the way I always tell it. It's my story in more ways than my little girl will ever know.

"Joni followed the music."

"Good idea," she says.

"It's always a good idea to follow the music," I say. "The music kept getting louder as she got closer, until she found herself at the park. She couldn't believe her eyes. It was like a circus had come to town."

Joni's head flops forward for a split second, then snaps back. Almost asleep. I lower my voice to a whisper. "People had painted their bodies with flowers and paisley swirls. Someone was blowing giant bubbles that floated over the park and shimmered in the sunlight. There was a big tall pole with a huge flag at the top blowing in the breeze. But there weren't stars and stripes or anything like that on the flag. Instead, there was a peace symbol…"

I tuck my locket under my sweatshirt and crane my neck to peer over the top of her head. Her eyes, more bronze than brown, flutter closed. She's out, or almost out.

"Were you there?" she says, without opening her eyes. The question stops my heart.

She's never asked that before.

I take a deep breath, stalling for time. "Sometimes it feels like I was."

She gathers Tusker, the narwhal, close. My mother knitted him out of heathered gray yarn when Joni was born. One of his eyes, stitched with purple thread, has frayed into a permanent wink.

"We need to have Grandma Di-Di fix this guy," I say softly, running the dangling thread between my fingers. (We pronounce it Die-Die. My mother's name is Diana. Her husband—not my father, but I could never call him my stepfather because…it's complicated…anyway—he calls her Di, like the princess. So Joni has called her Grandma Di-Di ever since she could call her anything.)

"No," Joni insists. "He doesn't want to be fixed. He likes not looking like all the other narwhals."

"He's very smart," I say.

"I think I want to be a narwhal for Halloween."

"Excellent choice," I say.

"And people gave each other beads," she says, opening her eyes, urging me on.

"They did."

"Like these." Joni reaches a chubby index finger toward her bedside table where a strand of beads dangles from the nightlight shaped like a moon. Her finger sets the beads swinging from the point of the crescent. They clank gently against the framed photo of Joni with her father. It was taken at Disneyland and Nathan is high-fiving Pluto. I wonder if there's a picture of me on the nightstand next to her bed at Nathan's house.

It's late and tomorrow's a school day, but I'm having a hard time pulling myself away from the smell of her hair—lavender, marshmallow, deep red berries. I peel myself off the bed, one vertebra at a time in order not to break the stillness. I love it here, on her bed with her, but it's my job to encourage sleep. A little girl needs plenty of rest to face the rigors of kindergarten (even TK, transitional kindergarten, that recently-branded bridge between pre-school and the kindergarten big time).

It's my job to know what Joni needs: a good nine hours of sleep, healthy food (without almond-momming or overdoing sugar restriction so that she can learn moderation), limited screen time (without banning it altogether—again, the moderation thing). I'm trying my best to get it all right all the time, which, I know, is a fool's pursuit, but I am that fool. Like the song says: that little light of hers, I'm going to make damn sure it shines. I paraphrase. Whatever. Parenting is exhausting. Who knew exactly how exhausting.

I kiss her forehead. "I love you."

"I know," she says. "You love me so much."

"I do, Jojo." I smooth the blanket under her chin. "I love you so much."

"Mommy?' she says. "Why did the door move to the pantry?"

"Why?"

"Because it wanted to be ajar."

I let out a snort.

"Get it? A. Jar."

"I get it. Good one."

"I made it up."

"You did?"

"Yes, I did."

"You're so punny," I say, adjusting her door to allow the requisite six inches of light from the hallway.

"Good one, Mommy."

As I head down the hall, I hear her muttering to herself, "Punny…punny…" She's taking the word out for a test drive.

I'd like nothing better than to flop onto the couch and watch *The Great British Baking Show*. I believe it's biscuit week. (It's worth tuning in just to luxuriate in their referring to cookies as biscuits.) I'm strictly a slice-and-bake girl—thank you, Pillsbury—but that show is my secret pleasure. It's not one bit trashy, so it can't qualify as a guilty pleasure, but it's secret nonetheless insofar as no one knows I watch it. Even when Nathan still lived here, he never knew. Or bothered to know. Maybe if we'd bonded over a *trompe l'oeil* showstopper—a cake that looked like a picnic basket, perhaps—we'd still be together. Unlikely.

I decide to allow myself one episode. The treadmill taunts me from the corner of the living room (which is basically the who-cares room, décor-wise, ever since Fisher-Price became the predominant color palette). That's the deal I've made with myself: treadmill time as atonement for mindlessly watching people bake. There's some weird calorie-in/calorie-out osmosis there, even if the calories in are entirely virtual.

It's been a sweats-and-ponytail kind of day, so I simply step onto the treadmill and power it up. Ever since the whole 12-3-30 craze, that's been my pre-set. Twelve percent incline, three miles per hour, thirty minutes. By now, my body knows exactly what three miles per hour feels like. My feet start moving at that pace of their own accord. My iPad rests on the little ledge built into the treadmill. I scroll through my email, then check my Insta feed as I turn on the mammoth flat screen mounted on the opposite wall.

In the interest of good citizenship, I check CNN and the rest of the news echo chambers. Ukraine. The Middle East. Sixty-six pounds of confiscated fentanyl. Talking heads debating points so perpetual as to be moot. The other Talking Heads knew the truth: same as it ever was.

I mute the TV and turn to my smaller screen. TikTok sucks me in. I watch JLo demonstrate a pumpkin spice latte makeup. Don't ask me why—why I watch and/or why the ubiquitous autumnal flavor has insinuated itself into the JLo glow. I pass on a super young wannabe influencer explicating a whole "contour situation." And another (I think she was a real housewife of somewhere or another) proclaiming an eyeshadow stick purchased in a drugstore—just imagine!—to be "at the level."

I can't imagine what algorithm I poked to deliver so much makeup content. A daily swipe of sunscreen—that's a full face of effort for me. How the Big Brother of the web matched me to these tutorials is a mystery.

I swipe past a middle-aged woman wearing chunky turquoise jewelry promising to help women "level up their communication."

No thanks. Being married to a psychologist scratched any self-improvement itch I might have had which, to be candid, never really blossomed into a full-blown itch, but stayed more like an allergic rash of self-awareness. Cohabitation with a Psych PhD had more than enough antihistaminic effect.

My eye lands on Nathan's book, prominently positioned in the bookcase. He left a copy there, facing forward like a "Staff Pick" in a bookstore, among all the other books' vertical spines. It's called *Force of Habit: The Past Need Not Dictate The Future.* We argued about the subtitle for weeks, maybe months. I winced at the phrase "need not." Could a less sexy pairing of words grace a book jacket? He insisted the book skewed toward scholarly tome as much as self-help book, so the phrase "need not" communicated precisely the right tone. Maybe we were already looking for reasons to argue.

Once, when I was eleven or twelve, I asked my mom why she'd spent an entire evening fighting with Dad over whether or not to serve the salad undressed and let each of us pick our own dressing at the table. She told me that by that point they were simply looking for things to fight about. I remember thinking that even if that were the case, they could have come up with something less mundane. (Personally, I felt strongly that salad should arrive at the table already dressed to compliment the meal, but I never weighed in. I fancied myself the Switzerland of domestic dysfunction.) I can't believe I ended up treading the same petty marital terrain. At my parents' level after all.

I shift my focus back to the television. CNN is running footage of a protest outside a bank in New York City. A cadre of climate defenders thrust their signs in the air: "Stop funding fossil fuel!"

I switch to Netflix in search of my British baking friends, but the new episode hasn't dropped. I try Apple +. The ghost of Steve Jobs has plenty of ideas for me: a series about tourists on electric bikes, another about video game development, and a documentary called *Show Me The Picture* about Jim Marshall, the madman rock 'n' roll photographer who shot the hell out of the sixties. Apple + knows me after all. Though I do wonder how. Again, the creepy algorithm thing. Photography—easy enough. But the sixties? How does it know? Some sort of AI mind meld? Nobody knows about my particular…shall we say, relationship…to the sixties. Nobody. It's my deep, dark secret. Whatever. Amending that: deep, but not dark—more like day-glo.

I'll have to wait for biscuit week.

I click on the documentary.

Less than a minute in, Marshall's cameras are piled willy-nilly on top of one another, among them a Leica very much like my own. My heart lurches. Cut to portraits on the walls of his house: Hendrix, McCartney, Grace Slick. The voice-over jolts me: "Let's talk about the Haight. You had Jimi there right in the middle of that, right in the middle of the whole Haight-Ashbury Summer of Love." Black-and-white photos of kids in the Haight, packed in the streets, swarming on a rooftop. I lean forward, straining to look for myself in the rapid-fire montage of photos of Haight-Ashbury, Summer 1967.

I'm not there. Of course not. Just the Grateful Dead. Jefferson Airplane. Big Brother and the Holding Company. There's Janis. There's Jerry. Jim and Jimi. They're all there. Of course they are. That was their time. But no shots of one hit wonders, bands that never hit the stratosphere. The world doesn't remember them, only their one song. Like 'Tamara Moonlight,' the one I was named for. And it was named for me. You might say that song sits at the nexus of a kink—*my* kink—in the time-space continuum. I guarantee that's a factoid Jim Marshall never knew.

My phone pings. I pause the doc. Incoming text from Nathan.

—*We might invite Caroline's niece to sleep over Sat.*

I stare at the screen. The ghost dots dance.

—*She's 8. K w/ u?*

—*Sure.*

He shoots back a thumbs-up.

That's part of the problem with being newly divorced from this guy. He's so decent. He didn't have to ask my permission. It's his weekend. He's got custodial carte blanche. He could, however, have left out the "we." Clearly the pronoun makes him giddy. He's part of a "we" again…already. Even so, he did a nice thing by asking. (That's the grown-up in me talking; she makes the very rare appearance.)

I resume the documentary.

There's a killer shot of the Airplane sitting in a tree, then one of The Dead giving the camera the finger. Then one of—I click off the TV. Those were the kinds of photos I was supposed to be taking. The vanguard of psychedelia may have given Jim Marshall the finger, but the vanguard of today's music was supposed to be giving *me* the finger. (Literally, not metaphorically, which—to torture a metaphor—is actually how things turned out for me professionally.)

Does today even have a vanguard? Certainly none who could duplicate the righteous indignation in Grace Slick's eye staring down a camera lens. Queen Bey? TayTay? You gotta love 'em, shoving women artists front and center and boosting the economy Jeff Bezos-scale. More power to them, but the times they have a-changed. If these current powerhouse women were going to give a photographer the finger, it would be after spending hours in hair and makeup and squeezing themselves into a hundred thousand dollars-worth of sequins. They might even do it with a pumpkin spice latte glow.

So not Grace Slick.

I rationalize (read: pretend) that it was my choice to backburner my rock photography dreams. I tell myself that musicians stopped trying to change the world and started trying to crack the Forbes 400. But there's more to it than that. It's complicated. Like marriage and motherhood and carrying inside you the memory of a time you visited when you were seventeen, a time before you were born…a memory that reminds you of the best version of yourself and of all the ways life chipped away at that version and left you with… well, you.

I stop the treadmill and step off. I wander down the hall to my bedroom. I still think of the bedroom as my parents' room. (Paging Dr. Freud.) That's what happens when your mother gives you her house, which my mother did when she moved from Marin County to San Francisco. At the time, techies were flooding the city, drawn by the siren song of cyber ka-ching. My mom couldn't resist bringing the expertise that made her the queen of Kentfield real estate to the city's Marina District and Pacific Heights. Besides, her new hubby Bob had roots in the Haight that couldn't quite reach out here to Marin. They bought a two-bedroom/two-bath condo in a highrise on Nob Hill. (It was advertised as a "testament to luxury living." She fell for the ad line as much as the place and figured if she was going to co-opt the phrase professionally, she might as well buy the co-op.) She made a more-than-decent living selling high-end homes to the invading techies, enough so that Bob could quit his day job teaching biology at a secondary school. Now he can take whatever session gigs come his way as a drummer. Or not. I reiterate: my mom does pretty well.

So Nathan and I moved into the old family homestead. Probably a mistake. We spent a rom-com weekend—the cheesy song montage sort of weekend—painting walls and restaining cabinets. We OfferUpped the furniture my mother left behind and replaced it with our own, an embarrassingly on-brand newlywed mix of Ikea and low-end West Elm. But family history lingered. It was still the house where my childhood went poof. Divorce can leave behind some strong juju.

Now that Nathan's gone, more than ever this bedroom has reverted to being my parents' room. I wander in. I peel off my sweats and throw on boxer shorts and a ratty No Doubt T-shirt. (There's irony there, considering "Doubt Everything" might as well be my personal motto.)

I lie in bed for a full twenty-seven minutes…but who's watching the time tick by, digits flipping one to the next? I officially give up on sleep and slide into my Ugg slippers to pad back down the hall to the darkroom, passing Joni's room along the way. I pause to listen to the rhythmic rumble of her petite snore. It's slightly more stuffy than usual. I hope she's not catching a cold. It's early October, right on target for the petri dish known as kindergarten to sprout any number of sinus miseries.

The darkroom is a converted powder room—tiny, but my special place. I wanted my own darkroom ever since I took up photography in middle school. Once I became a so-called professional, it seemed only fair that I have one, like I earned the privilege. I thought developing my own pictures would make me feel less of a fraud.

Photography was my profession, but I didn't feel like a professional. Hard to explain the chasm between those two semantic shores, but it was mighty deep. Its edges were pretty jagged, too.

"Professional" is a bizarrely charged word. Like my little girl, I like words, but unlike her—thank God for her sake—I tend to parse them for how they can betray you. I am, technically, a professional by virtue of the fact that I get paid to take pictures. Pictures of houses. Real estate photography—big whoop, as the "graders" say. (That's what Joni calls the older kids at school, who are basically everyone beyond kindergarten.) Big whoop, say I, now at the age of thirty-four.

My career—if that's what you get when you string together a series of jobs—began when my mom begged me to pinch hit for her regular guy. For eons, she used the same guy, Perry Something, to take her picture once a year. She'd have new brochures printed up and fork over the big bucks to plaster her face on the bus bench in front of the Half Day Café.

We go to the cafe a lot on Saturday mornings so Joni can order the "blubes." They're really just blueberry pancakes, but, again, it's a fun word, and after Monday through Friday of figuring out three meals a day, I'm ready for someone else to flip the blubes. So we go to the Half Day. And there's Grandma Di-Di on the front of a bus bench flashing a head-cocked smile, teeth so white they deserve an animated sparkle. Of course, no one in Kentfield rides the bus, so it's more like a take-a-seat billboard. It has crossed my mind that Mom greased a palm or two to get the city council to sign off on having something as *déclassé* as a bus bench in the heart of our pristine little town just so that she could use it for shameless self-promotion. As if there were any other kind.

So I took her picture. And then I shot a house she was selling. It turns out I have a knack for making staged houses look bigger, brighter, more alluring—the eager repositories of a prospective homeowner's vision of a blissful future. I'm not particularly proud of this knack. It's just a magic trick. Craft, not art. Not by a long shot—pun only semi-intended because, to be accurate, it's not a long shot, it's all about the wide-angle. The wide angle and the blue hour when the sun is below the horizon and the sky turns deep blue so that the lights inside the house look extra warm and glowy. As I said, it's all about the tricks. Mom swore my photos enticed buyers into houses in record numbers. She recommended me to everyone in her office. Within a few months, I found myself with something resembling a career. Mom said we made a great team—an assessment of our mother-daughter relationship that would have fallen into the highly unlikely category when I was growing up. Ah, the teen years.

I yearned for a darkroom, enamored with the idea of locking myself away under the red light of emerging photos. So romantic. Now I have one...even though the digital age has rendered it obsolete. Nathan pointed that out to me—more than once—but I played the *artiste*. I dug out my Leica and insisted it could achieve nuances its digital counterparts never could. Cropping, dodging, burning. Those were the tricks of my so-called trade. Making those things happen by pushing buttons could never be the same as breathing in the smell of chemicals and coaxing an image to ripple itself alive onto a blank piece of Ilford 8x10.

I've been avoiding the darkroom the last few days. Make that weeks. A month or two.

The photographs from Nathan's engagement shoot are still clipped to the cord strung above the trays of developer, fixer, and stop bath. Here's Nathan gazing into the limpid aquamarine eyes of the lovely Caroline. There, whispering something so funny into her pearl-studded ear that her eyes are closed in laughter. Clearly, Caroline is determined to tick every item on a first-time bride's must-have list. Hence the engagement shoot. (Needless to say, when Nathan and I got married, there was no engagement shoot.

As I recall, our attitude was more: we've seen each other survive the both-ends-at-once stomach flu, so we might as well get married.)

I had no particular desire to take these photographs. I have less desire to lay eyes on them again.

I don't know why I agreed to be my ex-husband's wedding photographer. But I can't back out. I'm nothing if not a woman of my word—historically, far too many words, generally each one of far too many syllables. "Sure" felt like the adult, sophisticated response when he asked me. Such a Nathan move. So very: we'll-be-better-friends-than-we-were-spouses. So civilized. So Noel Coward. I can't believe I agreed. I wanted to prove I was equally up for moving on. I needed to prove it, to myself more than to Nathan. He'd already moved on. Obviously. I told myself I want to be there to see Joni skip down the aisle, sprinkling rose petals (or whatever kind of petals the lovely Caroline chooses), but the truth is I need to see Nathan standing at the end of that aisle opposite someone whose salient feature is that she's not me. I need to see that in order to make the whole he's-moved-on thing real. Pathetically clichéd. Oh well, clichés become clichés for a reason. Happy to do my part.

Important to note that he kept his promises to me. He did. He was far too evolved to cheat on me. Cheating was incongruent with his self-image. When he sat me down, it was not to confess, but rather to give me his particular, psychologically-tilted version of the it's-not-you-it's-me speech. He told me he'd never imagined he had the temperamental makeup—he said that: "temperamental makeup"—to fall head over heels. "Besotted" was the word he used. And get this: besotted in a way he'd never experienced before. I remember all the words, every one of them. By nature and by training, he's a man who chooses his words carefully. He knows they have repercussions. Even so, I don't believe he knew how hard the subtext of his words would hit. This is what he was telling me: I, Tamara Caldwell, a.k.a Mari, had never made his heels somersault over his head. He had never been besotted with me.

As I unclip the photos and pile them on the worktable, the conversation floods back. Not exactly a conversation. More of a presentation. I'm surprised he didn't assemble a PowerPoint: here are all the ways our marriage was less than. Honestly, though, I didn't need a slide show. I knew all the ways. I was living them. I suppose I knew all along that there was something missing. But it hurt anyway, to discover that he knew it too. It was easier to manage the fact of our marriage's sorry-ness as my personal disorder—free-floating, but persistent, like the niggling, low-grade anxiety he spotted in me early on. Love at first diagnosis. Nathan Lockhart's version of love anyway.

Now, inside my darkroom, I resent being surrounded by Nathan-and-Caroline. I was an idiot to accept this gig. Why did I agree to the prospect of swirling paper through chemical soup, prodding it with tongs, to watch an image of Nathan and Caroline emerge? Why should I of all people be the one to capture the grand launch of their happily-ever-after? And what will all that do to my recurrent GERD? The answers are, respectively: idiot, idiot, and I might as well book a GI appointment right now.

I unclip the last photo. It's from the casual, hanging-out-in-the-park batch: Nathan gazing at Caroline as she ties her platform sneaker. I wonder if he ever looked at me that way when I wasn't watching him watch me. Are looks like that inevitably stamped with an expiration date?

In all fairness to Nathan, I could never quite dismiss the possibility that maybe I was comparing him…comparing us…to a past I dropped in on all those years ago, an unscheduled detour in that pesky time-space continuum. A visit that left me with nostalgia for a time that wasn't even mine.

I slip the photos into a folder and place it under my old Leica, running my fingers over the camera's dimpled surface as I lift it. I glance at the clock. One a.m. I have to get up in five hours. I could buy myself an extra ten or fifteen minutes if I pack Joni's lunch now, but it's a bogus bargain. Fifteen minutes at this end or that—what's the difference? At either end, fifteen minutes isn't enough to erase my undereye circles.

I head back to bed, wondering what Nathan would have said if I'd told him: when I was seventeen, I spent a few days in the Summer of Love, 1967.

CHAPTER TWO

I'm speeding through dense fog. My foot stomps on the brake. Nothing. No response. The pedal is made of mush. My car careens through the mist. Zero visibility. Then it appears—the Golden Gate Bridge. I stomp on the brake. Again. Again. The pedal dissolves. Faster, faster. Only acceleration. The bridge looms closer. The curtain of fog obscures everything. Airless. Suffocating. Jerking the steering wheel, but the car is out of control. On the bridge now, speeding faster, faster. Flashes of the city. It should be getting closer, but it keeps receding into the distance, out of reach. The bridge doesn't extend far enough. No reaching the other side. Telescoping in—faster, closer, faster, closer. The car flies off the edge. Ocean rushes up. Car plummets down.

In the sliver of air that hangs over the bay, I wake up.

I can't remember the last time I had the dream. It stalked my teenaged years, flaunting my fear of driving and etching my bridge phobia deeper and deeper into my psyche. One-stop-shopping dread. The OG nightmare.

I had the dream the night before my excursion to 1967. That morning, I jolted awake to the last day of junior year…to a face in the mirror that was still a work in progress…to a high school social scene that mocked me. Again: ah, the teen years.

Every time I've had the dream since, the bridge extended far enough. The two front wheels of the car lifted off the ground, but the two rear wheels remained on *terra firma*. Then the front wheels bounced back down onto the bridge, and I drove to the other side. Every time. My subconscious is not known for its subtlety.

I reach for yesterday's sweats jumbled on the chair in the corner. Too gross, even in these post-pandemic, who-cares times. I yank on a pair of jeans, lose the No Doubt shirt, and pull a boring sweater over my head.

"Mommy!"

Normally I rouse Joni with good morning songs and tickle fingers, but she's already up.

"What is it?" I call. I cross the hall to her room while slipping the elastic off my wrist and pulling my hair into a ponytail. These days a hair elastic always lives on my wrist, at the ready for one or the other of us, Joni or me.

She's standing in the middle of her room, legs a good foot apart. She wears her panda print sleep sack—a weighted item with holes for her arms and feet. It makes her look like a human teepee.

"What's up?" I say.

"Well, I had a little accident."

That hasn't happened in a long time.

"How did that happen?" I ask. Dumb, unenlightened question.

"Well," she begins. "I knew I had to go, and I was on my way to the bathroom, but..." she gestures toward her sleep sack which is pretty impossible to get out of. "It's a long story."

I start to unzip her but stop. My nose tells me we need to take this to the bathroom.

"I should have said it was a big accident," says Joni, "if you catch my drift." I swear this kid sneaks Humphrey Bogart movies in the middle of the night.

"Got it," I say. I'll have to google if poop regression signals broken home trauma.

She waddles into the bathroom while I rummage for the wet wipes.

It's 6:12 a.m. and we're already late.

I clean her bottom and hustle her back into her room where I present her with wardrobe choices. It's time consuming to constantly offer choices in her nearly five-year-old life: oatmeal or scrambled eggs; pastels or crayons; blue leggings under her pink dress or black leggings under the green. Time consuming and exhausting, but I'm committed to developing her sense of agency.

She chooses blue under green. Then she begs to wear the love beads to school. I don't have the bandwidth to argue. I slip the strand off the moon nightlight and hand it to her.

"Go ahead," I say, "but you have to promise to be super careful with them. They're very special to me." She understands that they pre-dated her. I myself have given up trying to understand: even though they were placed directly into my hands in real hippie time, they pre-dated me too.

She slides them over her head, going cross-eyed as she peers down at them resting on her chest. "This one's my favorite." She taps an oversized bead, ovoid in shape, and rolls it between her fingers. It's the one that reminds me of old-fashioned Christmas candy, the kind that has an intricate design imbedded in its center.

"How come they're called love beads?" she says.

"Well…because you give them to someone you love. And because you wish that person love. They're sort of a symbol."

"What does that mean?"

"That means…" I consider what it means as she tries to tie her shoelaces. My fingers twitch to help her, but I don't. Bunny ear loop with this lace…bunny ear loop with that lace…loop over loop… But no, the laces still dangle, untied. I raise my eyebrows, asking permission to take over. She shakes her head.

"I got this," she insists.

I'm proud of her perseverance, but we're going to be late for school. Late gives me a borderline migraine. My problem, not hers.

I start again. "A symbol is something that stands for something else. Like these beads…they stand for love…of course, they're called love beads… But they also stand for peace and people taking care of each other. They stand for unity."

"What's that?"

She raises her shoelaces, untied, toward me. I take over. "It's the idea that everyone's connected."

"Like a family," she says.

"Yes," I say, "like a family."

I smear sunflower butter on a piece of bread, jelly on another, slap them together, and drop the sandwich in her little Bento box along with some slices of dried mango and a "smush," one of those fruit-and-veggie squeezie pouches that take the curse off kale.

Joni can climb into her car seat on her own, but we're in a hurry so I lift her in. She's still fiddling with the beads as I clamp the buckle.

She wants to hear her favorite song from *Moana*, but I can't find it on my phone, so I sing instead (*"See the line where the sky meets the sea / It calls me…"*).

"No, Mommy! Not that part."

That's the only part I remember.

I turn on the Kids Place station on Sirius radio. Pharrell is urging us to *"clap along if you feel like a room without a roof."*

I glance into the rearview mirror. Joni's little palms are pumping, elbows out, like a mini teenager. I never do that. How does she know about raising the roof?

The song ends and segues into "Hot Dog, Hot Dog, Hot Diggity Dog." Joni sings as I drive past the post office on the right, then Woodlands Market on the left. I spent a lot of time in their bakery when Nathan did a gluten-free month.

I'm trying to recall which came first—the gluten-free era or the flexitarian—when I hear from the backseat: "Uh-oh."

Please may it not be another potty incident.

My eyes dart to the rearview mirror. One end of the strand of beads trails from Joni's neck. I don't have to look to know that beads have scattered across the backseat.

"I told you to be careful!"

Even in the mirror, I can see the tears puddling in her eyes.

"I'm sorry," she says.

"Sorry doesn't really help, does it?" I hate that tone of voice. It's the tone I swore I'd never use.

"I'll find them all," she says.

"You have to go to school." I try for a deep breath. "I'll find them."

The tears spill over, splashing down her cheeks. She doesn't bother to wipe them away. She's crying too hard. Her breath catches in syncopated shivers, those tremulous little pants that break my heart.

"It's okay," I lie. "You should never cry over something that can't cry over you."

"I'm not," she insists between strangled breaths. "I'm crying for you. Because they're one of your favorite things. And mine too. Both of our favorite. They're going to be all mixed up. They'll never be the same."

By the time we arrive at school—not late, but teetering on migraine—Joni's managed to gather up a fistful of beads. I open the back door. She hands them to me gingerly so as not to let any slip between her fingers, even though most of them still lie strewn across the backseat, buried along with petrified Cheerios in the crevices of her car seat or rolled into the dark abyss under the driver's side.

"Thank you," I say. She transfers them from her hand to mine as though they are the most precious jewels. I stuff them into the pocket of my jeans.

She looks up at me. "We can fix them, right?"

"Absolutely." I kiss the top of her head. "Remember," I add, unbuckling her. "Daddy's picking you up today and you're going to spend the weekend with him. You're going to have so much fun."

"I remember."

She's got the routine down pat. She's not the only kindergartner with rotating weekends, but she's my kindergartner. My baby with two households, which are definitely not twice as good as one. (Nathan and I considered, momentarily, birdnesting, that most recent of splitsville protocols in which the child stays put and the two parents come and go in and out of the "domicile," but since the domicile in question happens to be my childhood home, that seemed untenable. Not that tenability counts for much when you're playing 52 pickup with your child's life.)

"Actually," I say, "it's a long weekend."

"How can a weekend be long? A weekend is always two days."

"A long weekend is when you have no school on Monday. So you get to play with Daddy an extra day."

"Got it."

"I love you," I say, hugging her—extra tight, an extra second. It's going to be three days before I can tell her that in person again.

"I know," she says. "You love me so much." Then she skips into school. Literally. Skipping is a newly acquired skill, like snapping her fingers, and she can't get enough. After a few skips, she misses a beat, pauses to reset, and starts again. Joni's BFF, Ava, joins in, matching her rhythm.

Ava is the daughter of my old high school classmate, Vanessa. Through a vexing quirk of fate, Joni has ended up in a class with the children of my nemesis clique from high school. The most annoying part of that scenario is knowing that I've been cruising along the exact same life track as these girls, almost year for year. But I'm the only one divorced so far. Whoopee for me.

I worry that Ava has her mother's elitist DNA and that Joni will be left in the dust within a few short years. But today, they're skipping holding hands, just because you automatically hold hands with your friend.

Mr. Chappell stands at the school door greeting each kid, sometimes with a high-five, sometimes a fist bump, or even a dance step. One morning—now the stuff of legend—he had the whole kindergarten doing the electric slide. The weirdest part was picturing aging hippie Mr. Chappell electric-sliding his way through a disco phase.

When I was in high school, Mr. Chappell taught sophomore Composition. And my junior elective: Photography. I prided myself on my eye, but he made it his mission to challenge me. He thought I had talent and made me suffer for it. He was that kind of teacher, the kind who force you to achieve your potential. When I see him now, every morning at drop-off, I sense his disappointment in me. It's like a thought bubble appears over his head, saying, "You're an artist, not a salesman." He's never said a word, of course. I'm not even sure he knows I take pictures to sell houses. But I picture his disappointment like the cloud of dust that hovers around that *Peanuts* character.

Real life has caught up with both of us, Mr. Chappell and me. He went out of his way to teach me to get up-close and personal with my photographic subject, and now I'm taking pictures of rooms to make them look as big and impersonal as possible. Meanwhile, he segued from inspiring recalcitrant kids like me to becoming a school administrator, now aged-out into being a gray-haired elementary school Walmart greeter.

I lean into the backseat to hunt for the rest of the beads. It's an archaeological dig. I extract an old Starbucks cup, two wrappers from organic granola bars, and three stray socks belonging to Joni, no two a pair. I unearth a bead wedged behind the padded headrest of Joni's car seat, but it turns out to be a raisin.

When I stand up, I find myself face to face with that gaggle of girls who have plagued me since sixth grade. Women now, but the same old girls to me. We've all ended up in the parking lot of our hometown elementary school shuttling kids. (See "downbuzz" in urbandictionary.com.)

Their pecking order hasn't changed. Vanessa is still the queen bee. The others reside in her shadow. Rachel, still the nice one, turns to me.

"What are you thinking about middle school?"

"I try to think about those halcyon days as little as possible," I say. "I haven't even replaced the burnt-out neon in the sign that said DORK across my forehead."

Rachel titters. Over the years she's learned that's the safe and suitable reaction to anything I say.

Vanessa slides her sunglasses to the top of her highlighted hair. "For Joni?"

"Oh!" I say. "Of course. JK." It's nauseating how quickly I vomit eighth grade jargon when I'm clique-adjacent, even expressions like "JK" that I personally never used in eighth grade.

Amanda rattles off the names of several private schools. Her voice rises after each one like it's a self-contained question. I don't know if she's asking whether I'm considering them or simply if I've ever heard of them. I shrug. I've been so focused on getting Joni through kindergarten unscathed by our divorce that I haven't given a thought to what happens beyond tomorrow, let alone fifth grade. Bad mother.

Amanda's wide eyes suggest she's poised for one of my rambles. But I've left those behind. Or tried to. In the interest of self-control. I haven't succeeded one hundred percent, but I'm a solid B-plus. When a ramble slips out these days—more like spews out—it's either because I'm flustered and embarrassed (the double-header of mortification) or because I'm so at ease that control is a moot point. Self-aware much? I shrug again.

Kelly, the last of the four horsewomen of my social apocalypse, arrives toting a cardboard coffee carrier. Four perfectly purchased Starbucks orders, down to the sugar-free vanilla and the coconut milk foam.

"Hi, Mari, how are you?" she says as she hands them out. "You'll have to tell me your order for next time."

She has asked me before. I've told her before. More than once. It's pretty easy. Black with a dash of cream—the kind that comes from a cow.

Amanda rests her coffee on the hood of her Range Rover and pulls out her phone. "Payback moment?" She taps the screen.

Vanessa and Rachel do the same. Tap, tap. Opening Splitwise. Tap, tap, tap. Kelly is instantly paid back. Four girls sharing one hive mind.

I hold out my hands, palms up, revealing a treasure trove of backseat garbage and head for the trash can.

I'M DUE AT THE home of a tech scion at ten o'clock to meet up about shooting his house. He's owned it less than a year, but the sun doesn't hit the swimming pool at the right time of day. What's a guy to do but sell? He's twenty-four years old. As in: ten years younger than I am. You might say we have different priorities. I've postponed the meeting twice. Third time's the now-or-never.

I head home to change into something a little more respectable, like my better jeans and a sweater without pills. I sing along to "Baby Shark" in the car for a chorus, then switch to MSNBC. I'm beyond disgusted with politics, but like a nervous flyer who must remain alert to keep the plane in the sky… Let me double-click on that: I'm convinced the country will crash and burn if I don't have a passing familiarity with the news. It's one of those unanticipated side effects of parenthood that no one warns you about. Not only do I have to keep my baby safe *right now*, I have to keep her safe forever and leave her a decent world if at all possible (which seems less and less likely).

Before I can hear the latest bad news, Sarah calls. My oldest friend and, by default, my best friend. No need for hellos.

"Vanessa Winthrop sends her regards," I say.

"To *moi*?" says Sarah, feigning delight. It's our routine. We pitch our tent in the us-against-them camp.

"Yes," I vamp, "she made a special point."

"What's she up to?" says Sarah.

"The usual. Being cringe."

"It's like time stood still."

"I know," I say. "I can't believe I have to see the girly-girls all the time. What karma am I still paying off?" I consider stopping for coffee out of spite since Kelly's coffee run left me out, but I keep driving.

"What're you doing this weekend?" She knows it's Nathan's weekend with Joni. Her voice lilts just like it used to when we were kids and it was my weekend to be with Dad but chances were he was going to flake out. It was a loaded question then. It's a loaded question now. Her cheerful lilt still takes the curse off.

"I don't know." I honestly have no idea. "It's a three-day weekend, too. Some sort of school in-service day."

"Wow!" I can hear Sarah's brain click into hyperdrive. "You've got to do something fun. Something spontaneous."

"I can't do spontaneous. I'm a parent."

"You never did spontaneous," she points out. "Come on. Go somewhere. I wish I could go with but I've got to finish a brief."

Every time she says something lawyerly, I'm walloped by the weirdness of life. I went to Yale and followed my so-called passion—photography—into oblivion, a.k.a. real estate work. Meanwhile, she went to a state school and now she's a fancy attorney writing briefs.

"How about Paso Robles?" says Sarah.

"What about it?"

"For your weekend getaway?"

"Did you just use the word 'getaway?'"

"Guilty," she says. "But Paso Robles is cool… How about Sonoma? Wine? Lots and lots of wine?"

"Not fun."

"A nice spa? Wraps and scrubs and facials…"

"Have you met me?"

"I'm serious," she says. "A deep-tissue massage could work wonders."

"I don't like to be touched by people I don't know. No. I think I don't like to be touched by people who don't know me. Conundrum, huh?"

Sarah lets out a protracted "hmmm." It's the sound of her giving up. "You're overdue for your post-divorce fling."

"Hurts right here," I groan. Something we've been saying to each other since we were twelve, meaning: *I'm laughing so hard, my side hurts*—to be used exclusively when something warrants absolutely zero laughter.

"You're your own worst enemy, you know," says Sarah. "I'd kidnap you but I've got deadlines. My first free weekend, consider yourself kidnapped."

"No one would pay the ransom."

"Pshaw," she says. She hits it hard—the "p" and the "shaw."

Another call rings through. GRANDMA DI-DI appears on the screen. "It's my mom."

"Tell her I say hi," says Sarah and clicks off.

"Sarah says hi."

"Hi Sarah," says Mom. She knows Sarah's not actually in the car. Their calls often overlap.

"How's my little girl?"

"Fine, just a little tired."

Conspicuous silence.

"Oh. You mean Joni."

"I like knowing how you are too."

"Joni's great," I say. "How's Bob?"

I spot an errant bead on the floor in front of the passenger seat.

"Having a bad day," says Mom. "One of his old bandmates died."

I'm stopped at a light and try to reach for the bead without taking my foot off the brake.

"From the band…" Mom goes on, "…that had that hit."

I graze the bead with my fingertip, sending it rolling farther away.

"Oh wait... Of course you know that song," Mom chatters. "It's your song. The song we named you after."

I'm mid-reach to the bead, bent sideways to keep an eye on the road, sort of. I freeze. "What did you say?"

"The song you were named after. 'Tamara Moonlight.'"

"One of those guys died?" I don't ask which one. I don't want to know.

"It kind of makes my head spin every time I think about it," says Mom. "That it was our song, mine and Dad's, and then we named you after it, and then I end up marrying Bob who was actually in the actual band."

I say nothing. Too many thoughts ricocheting against the inside of my skull. Mostly one: don't let it be Jimmy.

"Weird, right?" says Mom. "Like woo-woo cosmic weird."

"Yeah," I say. "So weird."

Mom natters on. "You remember that night I met Bob. In Napa? You and Nathan and me? Bob was in that band..."

"Neon Dream."

"Right," she says. "Neon Dream. You do remember."

Of course I remember.

NATHAN AND I HAD BEEN living together for a couple of years and we already had traditions. That felt good, stable—like what I needed at twenty-five. One of those traditions was taking a bike trip through wine country in the spring. When my mother finally broke up with her jerky post-Dad boyfriend, Nathan suggested inviting her along. Kind of weird—asking your mom to be a third wheel on a bicycle trip (would that make it a tricycle trip?) but we did and she said yes.

On the second night, one of the wineries hosted a concert. "Flashback: One Hit Wonders!" Groups from Mom's era. She said we didn't have to go, but of course we did.

I had a punchline for every band. Did Quicksilver Messenger Service need one of those motorized scooters to make deliveries? Did Strawberry Alarm Clock hit the snooze button? As for Electric Prunes—that name served up geriatric puns on a silver platter.

Snark came easy with all those aging rockers who strapped guitars in front of sizable paunches and lost track of the lyrics. Not to mention the issue of the hair. Once the defining emblem of their generation—*"Gimme a head with hair / Long, beautiful hair"*—it was now gray…or gone.

We were thinking about calling it a night (as opposed to what, I've always wondered) when the emcee stepped to the mic. "Ladies and gentlemen…Neon Dream."

I stared at the stage. Jimmy Westwood strode to the front. There he was. In person. Yanked from the recesses of a lucid dream. I squinted to find my Jimmy in that Jimmy. He was in there. And he still had it—charisma, the X factor, whatever the force that charged the atmosphere around him. Even though he had to be…what?…in his sixties?…late sixties?…there was no paunch, very little gray. All Jimmy Westwood—flashes of the young guy who drove me across the Golden Gate Bridge; who took me to a Be-In; who quieted the brain chatter that flew out of my mouth unfiltered. Who deflowered me. Jimmy Westwood was the guy who took it upon himself to settle my mind and ended up cracking open my heart. There he was, decades older while I was only seven years older. How was that possible? The mathematics of time travel or of the imagination? Of projection or delusion?

The other guys were there too. P.J. and Boo-Boo. Boo-Boo, a.k.a. Bob, would meet my mother that night and become my stepfather. Cue brain explosion. Sam wasn't there. Maybe he was living an idyllic life somewhere with his family, Jennifer and their daughter, Tomorrow. I was there the night Tomorrow was born, the night of the Battle of the Bands at The Fillmore, the night Neon Dream broke onto the scene. Now, Tomorrow must be an adult…

older than me? Maybe Sam wasn't interested in old times. When were those old times exactly? And how did it happen that I had landed there, kerplunk, in those times that belonged to those guys, not to me?

When I finally caught my breath, Nina was at the microphone with Jimmy. My memory of her had receded by then, gone all blurry as if my subconscious were protecting her identity on a true crime show, pixelating her into an amorphous non-entity.

"Remember that night?" my mom says again. I've given up on reaching the bead. I stare at the traffic light.

Yes, Mom, I remember that night.

The night I realized Jimmy and Nina were still together after all that time. The night I was reminded of how their son, James, was the perfect cross between them—the chisel of Jimmy's jaw, the slant of Nina's cheekbone.

There's a lot to wrap my head around when I think about James. How I met him the day I returned from 1967. How he was my boyfriend before Nathan. The two of them—that's the extent of my romantic history (if you don't count James's father, Jimmy, which sometimes I do and sometimes I don't depending on how strongly I believe I actually traveled through time. A belief that fluctuates wildly on any given day). James has crossed my mind several times in the past months. I make sure he does exactly that—cross, *just passing through*—and doesn't take up residence.

I try not to dwell on James. I don't aways succeed.

Especially now that Nathan and I are officially exes. A few months ago, Joni drew a picture of a monster, a ghost, and a cauliflower. Then she drew an "X" over them all in red crayon and taped the paper to her bedroom door—a highly efficient form of cancel culture. I picture a big red "X" scrawled across our marriage certificate, Nathan's and mine.

I hermetically sealed my relationship with James in its own little bubble, managing to avoid meeting his parents, Jimmy and Nina, the whole time we were together. I mean, seriously, how would that have gone? *"Nice to meet you, boyfriend's parents. Remember me? From long before your son, my boyfriend, was born? And by the way, boyfriend's dad, you were my first."* I managed to avoid such a meeting again that night in Napa at the One Hit Wonder concert. I stared at the stage, heart pounding as I stood between my mother and my boyfriend who, even then, I knew would become my husband. Nathan was such a grown-up. Wasn't that what you were supposed to want in a husband?

MY HANDS GO SLIPPERY, losing their grip on the steering wheel, as the light turns green.

"So," my mom says, "the memorial's going to be Monday at his house in the Haight. That Jimmy guy. The singer. I mean, he was the singer. Now he's gone. I guess he never moved."

"Sorry, Mom, I've got to go."

I pull over to the curb and double at the waist, my head resting against the steering wheel.

An MSNBC pundit argues, "The Supreme Court justices are appointed for life to the judiciary, not necessarily to the Supreme Court itself..." I switch to the satellite sixties station.

The deejay is into his spiel. "...It may not be a name a lot of you know, but you know the song. 'Tamara Moonlight.' The stuff of rock 'n' roll myth. A group signs up for a Battle of the Bands at the legendary Fillmore Auditorium in San Francisco. They're just one of many groups playing that night. All with big dreams. But this band belongs to a guy named Jimmy Westwood. They call themselves Neon Dream and the song they do that night is 'Tamara Moonlight.' They win the contest. The prize just happens to be a record deal. The song hits big, shoots up the charts, and then...that was it. The beginning and the end. What people like me call a 'one hit wonder.' But what a one-hit. It's a song that's on anybody's list of songs that made the sixties the sixties. A folk-rock ballad as good as the best of them. Written by Jimmy Westwood…a huge talent and from what everyone always says, one of the good guys. A lot of legendary artists are up there waiting for you to jam, Jimmy. Here's to you."

I close my eyes and listen. I know the opening riff as well as I know my own heartbeat—simple, dreamy, repetitive guitar lulling me in. Tambourine on the downbeat, one single tap, no frilly jingle-jangle. The drums, slightly muffled, from the distant shores of consciousness. Jimmy's voice, golden-throated, warm.

"*Tonight… I know that being with you was meant to be / Tonight… I look into your eyes, my soul I see…*"

Nina's voice slides in. There's the magic. In those two voices together. Nina's and Jimmy's.

"*Loving you is easier than breathing can be / Touching you, all the mysteries of life make sense to me…*"

I open my eyes. Ahead of me lies the rest of my day. The tech scion. The giant house with glass walls and concrete floors. The swimming pool in too much shade. I don't want to go there. I grip the wheel and make a U-turn for the city. And I head toward the bridge.

An arsenal of tricks now allows me to cope with my bridge phobia and drive the Golden Gate. I stay in the middle lane so no pesky edges flicker at my peripheral vision. I keep the AC blasting so I can dry my sweaty palms. I sing at the top of my lungs so I don't have to listen to the scary words in my brain. Joni calls it "Funny Bridge Mommy." I wonder how long it will take before she realizes it's Neurotic Bridge Mommy. Her father's a shrink. He'll help her unpack that.

I'm in the middle lane and the AC is blasting, but I can't sing. Not that song. Not with Jimmy gone. It never occurred to me that Jimmy would be so much older now. It never occurred to me that he could die.

Suddenly, I feel seventeen again...and, at the same time, so painfully grown up. Growing up is like driving the bridge writ large—curating a bunch of behaviors that let you live some semblance of a normal life, little disguises that keep you from looking like you're one heaping pile of fears. Tricks (I refuse to call them "life hacks") that vaccinate you against the overwhelm, which, let's face it, has become so...well, overwhelming...that we've had to turn it into an actual thing.

I put the song on repeat.

I approach the end of the bridge. Just this once I dare look up toward the city. It's one of those crystalline fall mornings, the Transamerica Pyramid piercing a cloudless azure sky.

CHAPTER THREE

Coming off the bridge, I merge to the right onto the elevated highway, the cypress and eucalyptus thick in the Presidio up ahead. I stop at a red light. A delivery robot rolls by, its red flag blowing in the breeze. Another one, with a different logo and a yellow flag, pauses at the intersection, then forges ahead. They jockey around one another in a little *you go/no, you go* maneuver.

I plug my destination into the GPS: The Fillmore. I hadn't thought about where I was going while I was on the bridge, drawn like a zombie to the other side. But now I know. I'm going to The Fillmore to soak up whatever molecules of the sixties might still be floating around there.

I wend my way through the city and turn onto Geary, heading toward Fillmore. The building is on the corner, the same Italianate brick box I remember.

I gaze into the arched windows and try to make out the crystal chandeliers that once hung inside. I have no idea if they're still there. I never went back after that fateful Battle of the Bands. Never in my normal twenty-first century life.

I need to go inside. I need to remember Jimmy on stage there. I circle the block looking for parking. No spots. It's against my principles to pay the highway robbery required to park in a lot in this city, so I broaden my circle, widening by additional blocks with each pass. No spots.

I might as well forget this nonsense and head home. But I find myself in the Haight. Quirky boutiques and retro-psychedelic murals. Is the neighborhood trying to pay homage to its roots or cash in on them? Two versions on a theme?

At least Amoeba Music still anchors the hood. Surely this is the day to buy another copy of Neon Dream's only record. I spot a BMW pulling out of a spot on the next block. I pull in and step out of the car. I'm nearly mown down by an e-scooter as I head down the sidewalk.

"Watch where you're fuckin' goin', lady," yells the scootee.

I'm equally offended by his jerkiness and by being called "lady."

A few empty storefronts dot the street between places selling turmeric shots and Janis Joplin lunch boxes. Places primed to give tourists the vibe they come for. A guy hawks decals and buttons from a kiosk. *Save the Earth, Women's Liberation, Stay Woke, Introverted but Willing to Discuss Cats.* Let's do the time warp again.

There's a diner that looks sort of familiar…but also not. I stare and stare until it dawns on me. It's the place where Jimmy and the band took me when I first landed out of time, the place with Love Burgers for twenty-five cents or for free if you couldn't manage the quarter. I step inside.

Most customers sit at tables alone with their laptops. They scan the menu's QR code on their phones.

I could use a cup of coffee. I remember that coffee, luxurious with real cream and served in a heavy crockery mug. I look for a server to order a coffee to go, but there's none to be found. Oh well.

Besides, the news of Jimmy's death has my heart knocking against my chest as though I'd already had five cups. Not my favorite sensation, this cardiac salsa. *Jimmy Westwood's dead…Jimmy Westwood's dead…* I step outside for some air.

This version of the Haight bewilders me. Every time I've come here since my visit at seventeen, I've shoved those Summer of Love memories to a cubby at the back of my brain. Today, I cannot. Did that diner ever have a life as the Love Burger joint? Did I invent loving Jimmy Westwood? Was my visit to the sixties a fever dream?

I've studied a lot about dreams in the intervening years. I know all about the continuity hypothesis, the theory that tells us our dreams are reflections of our waking thoughts. (Duh.) In my seventeen-year-old days, my waking thoughts had an awful lot to do with escaping myself: self-proclaimed—and, embarrassingly, self-aggrandized—outcast. It's totally possible I whisked myself into the sixties in my own mind.

I better whisk myself back to my life. I should call the tech heir and reschedule our meet-up.

I'm sliding my phone out of my back pocket as I round the corner and spot a VW van covered in painted flowers and multi-colored swirls—a psychedelic relic. I wander over. The doors are swung open. I step closer and crane my neck to peek inside. As I lean in, I trip over something. It's the homeless man in a heap in the gutter.

"I'm sorry, so sorry," I say as I tumble into the van. My head meets the door jamb with a thud, but I catch myself, one hand on either side of the opening. I don't fall. I'm okay.

"Oops," says a voice inside the van. The darkness of the interior is exaggerated by the noonday sun outside. "You okay?"

"I'm okay," I say, stepping in out of the glare.

It takes a second for my eyes to adjust. There's a guy lolling on the backseat. He wears wildly flared bellbottoms and a fringed vest. A leather cord is tied around his forehead. His hair hangs to his shoulders in waves.

Oh shit. Here we go again.

"How'd you get here?" he asks.

"Well," I say, "that's an interesting question to put it mildly. I have a history with…shall we say…sliding through worm holes or is it black holes? One of those speculative constructs that seem to provide me…I don't know…maybe other people too…with some sort of shortcut through time and space. Personally, I like to call it spacetime."

"That rap got you past the guard?"

"What guard?"

"The guy protecting the set."

"The set?"

"We're shooting a commercial."

I poke my head outside. A few crew members scurry about. The guard must be the guy emerging from a porta-potty zipping up his fly. He saunters toward the van.

"Where's the camera?" I wonder.

"Drone," he says.

I nod. "So this isn't the sixties?"

"Not as far as I know." He scrolls through his phone.

"Sorry to bother you," I say.

"No worries."

I pause. "What are you selling?"

"Supplemental Medicare insurance."

Of course.

I nod again and back out of the van. The guard ushers the homeless guy away. He heads down the street eating a donut and pushing an overstuffed shopping cart, struggling to keep its pyramid of belongings from toppling. I know the feeling—metaphorically, of course.

I head in the opposite direction.

Again, I pass boutique after boutique, all niched as vintage or relic. I glance into the window of Love on Haight to see a kaleidoscope of tie-dye. A sign in the window boasts their Women in Prison Reentry Tie-Dye Program. Maybe their slogan should be "From License Plates to Leggings." Maybe not. There's a tattoo and piercing parlor called Pin & Ink. An IPA brew pub, an upscale head shop, and the inevitable sushi bar. The Haight is eager to straddle eras. I feel myself sinking into the gap between them.

I continue down the block, past nondescript storefront after storefront when suddenly my breath catches. Something stops me: the remnants of an image once painted on the plate glass. The passing of time, ravages of weather, and attempts to scrape it off have nearly erased the image, but it's still there: a giant camera. A Leica like mine. Like the one I gave to Vic for safekeeping, knowing he would give it to my father, his son…who would give it to me.

It's complicated.

I stare at the ghost of the image.

This was it. Vic's camera shop.

I've been so obsessed with Jimmy's death that I haven't thought about the other person I left behind seventeen years ago. My grandfather. Vic. He never knew he was my grandfather, but I knew. I'd figured it out. I'd wanted to tell him. I tried to tell him without telling him. But I didn't want to blow our connection by having him think I was completely insane.

Vic's neighborhood camera shop, right here on this spot, now appears to be an Amazon pick-up center. The ghost of the Leica on the front window conjures Vic's face in my mind's eye: the almost cleft in his chin, the bushy eyebrows, the look of earnestness when he told me that being there for the people who mean something to you is all that matters.

I step inside. There's a service counter at the far end, but the room is mostly lined with lockers, each with a digital keypad. Signs all over the place explain how to use the facility while cameras point down from the ceiling, making sure everyone behaves. Those are the only cameras in sight. No Canons, no Nikons, no Leicas. No Vic. I exhale, deflated. I don't have to do the math to know he's long gone.

For the briefest moment, I get a whiff of a lingering metallic scent: hydroquinone and sodium carbonate. Could the odor still haunt Vic's darkroom in what was his little apartment upstairs? I wander toward the back of the store.

The guy behind the counter eyes me suspiciously. He's wearing Amazon blue and orange. The perky Amazon arrow darts across the pocket on his chest. "Can I help you?" he says, no hint of a smile to mimic that arrow.

"No," I say. "I used to know the guy who owned the store here a million years ago."

He doesn't care. Nostalgia clashes with Amazon's brand.

I head out and round the corner onto Masonic. When I was here before, there were back stairs that led up to Vic's apartment. I head for them. They're still there, on the side of the building a couple of feet from the building next door.

I climb up.

I remember the door at the top, peeling red paint in swaths. Now it's painted black. My heart does a little flip thing as I grasp the doorknob. I fully expect it to be locked. It's not. I open the door and go in.

I step directly into the tiny kitchen. All of Vic's stuff is gone, of course—his cookie jar collection long ago consigned to Goodwill, if not the garbage. You can tell right away that it's an office kitchen. The only appliance on the counter is a coffee maker. A small card table holds a coffee-stained mug and a Trader Joe's bag bearing a Post-it: Ken's.

I step into the living room. Actually, it's just *the room* since it's the only other room besides the miniscule bathroom and Vic's closet of a darkroom. But no one's doing anything resembling bona fide living in here. It's an office now. Ikea desks, ergonomically friendly chairs, one balance ball. A healthy smattering of charging outlets, USB hubs, and cables. All this in the space that once held a ratty yellow sofa and old person tchotchkes, souvenirs from Vic's life. I assume it's the office for the Amazon staff, but who knows? It could be some random office for some random start-up since that's exactly what it looks like: the shot in a documentary that depicts the humble beginnings of a couple of nerds who founded a gazillion dollar tech empire.

Where Vic's prize-winning black and white photographs once hung, the walls are blank except for a flowchart that covers half a wall.

I'll never visit this apartment again.

I turn to take one last look before leaving, straining to envision it as it used to be, filled with Vic's memories, filled with Vic. And then…the red light flickers on above the darkroom door.

I hadn't noticed that the light was still there, but it is. And suddenly it's on. Maybe the flowchart tech wannabes use the darkroom for something nefarious and the red light is some sort of signal. Maybe the wiring, like the rickety staircase, never got updated and goes on the fritz every now and then. There are all kinds of explanations, but for some inexplicable reason, I'm compelled to find out.

I knock lightly on the darkroom door.

Nothing.

I raise my hand to knock again but think better of it. What if there's a real photographer at work? I wouldn't want to interrupt someone in the zone. I can't believe I knocked in the first place. Dumb.

I glance up at the light, soft yet vivid, the unique red that's both a warning and a beacon. Clearly, I can wax nauseatingly poetic about darkrooms if given half a chance, and this gives me exactly that—only half a chance, because just like that, the light goes off. That old poltergeist wiring.

I open the door to see if the old equipment is still in there.

It is.

And so is Vic.

"Hi there, hon."

I stare at him. He's wearing the same gray cardigan with the same hole in the sleeve; the same thick eyeglasses make his same brown eyes look like M&M's; the same bushy caterpillar eyebrows arch above those eyes. He's exactly…the same. No older (which seems a lot younger to me now than it did then).

"It's been a little while," he says.

My mouth goes cotton dry.

"Everything hunky-dory?" he prompts.

I manage a nod.

"You remember me?" I say.

"My friend with the Leica," he says. "I've been taking good care of it."

"How long has it been?"

"Since what?"

"Since I was here?"

"Oh, I don't know. What do you think? Couple months. It was summer, right?"

"Of '67, right?"

"Right-o," he says.

I'll do my best not to appear as dense as I did when I first landed in… OMG… I'm in 1967… Again.

I reach for the locket that has slipped under my sweater. It's there, against my chest. Nathan gave it to me when Joni was born. It's still there, her birth date inscribed on the back, her picture safe inside…I hope.

I break out in a cold sweat. Acid rises in my esophagus. I might throw up. Time travel motion sickness. Whoa.

"You okay, honey?"

I nod again. "You recognize me?"

"Of course."

"I don't look older? Like, a lot older?"

"I know at your age, every little thing that happens makes you feel older. Just wait till you're my age," he chuckles. "Of course, please don't mistake me for an adult based on my current…status." He smiles broadly. The lines spraying out from the corners of his eyes crinkle under his glasses.

"How old would you say I am?" I ask.

"I make it a practice never to guess a lady's age," says Vic, "but since you told me you were seventeen a couple of months ago, I'm going to go with seventeen. Unless you had a birthday?"

"What month is it?" I ask.

"October."

"Then no," I say. "No birthday."

He picks up a Polaroid picture. The surface emulsion has been scraped and swirled. He trims off the border with tiny scissors. "You okay, kiddo?"

I nod and manage a deep breath. I'm smacked by the vinegar smell of the stop bath and the rotten egg odor of the fixer. That must be it. The occupational hazard of exposure to toxic chemicals has finally gotten to me. My brain has been pickled. "What's happening?" I say. *To me?*

"I'm just doing a little lift and transfer," says Vic. "Experimenting with Polaroids." He sets about transferring the image to a small canvas. "You kids think you invented psychedelic?" he says, chuckling again.

"Kids?" I say.

"Enjoy it while it lasts," he says.

How can I do that? My teenage years are over, no matter how I appear to Vic. On the inside, I'm my thirty-four-year-old self: someone's ex, someone's mother. The mother of Vic's great-granddaughter.

My hand flies to my back pocket to grab my phone. I need to show Vic a picture of Joni, but I realize that my phone-that's-so-much-more-than-a-phone is a magical techno bridge-too-far to explain. I reach for my locket again.

"Can I show you something?" I say.

"Sure thing."

I slip my fingernail into the little groove and flick it open. There's Joni, age two, apple dumpling cheeks and wisps of hair gathered into a fountain spouting from the top of her head.

"That you?" he asks.

I take a beat. There's no way to explain. Turns out I don't have to.

"You were a cutie pie," Vic continues. "Still are." It's not one bit creepy when he says it. He has no creep in him whatsoever. "A person could love that little girl."

I snap the locket closed. "You would," I say before I can stop myself.

I pick up the canvas with the transferred image from the Polaroid. The emulsion has been scraped into spirals, but I can still make out the subject: a neon sign. The red letters that spell out the name have been stretched into points and the Chinese characters beneath form one continuous design, but I know what it says: Sam Wo Restaurant—Chow Mein—Noodle. It's a legendary spot, but to me, it's the place where Jimmy and I went the night that changed my life.

"Cool."

"Thanks. Sometimes art is all about playing," he says. "No matter how old you are." He nods toward the canvas. "So I gotta get back to my playtime."

"I really want to see how it turns out," I say, setting the canvas on the worktable.

"Me too," he says. "But the not knowing is the fun part."

I edge toward the door. I have no idea what awaits on the other side. Vic stops me. "Hold on, kiddo." He picks up my camera, the Leica I left with him four months ago (or, depending on your timeframe, nearly sixty years ago). He hands it to me. "This belongs to you."

Its pebbly surface is familiar, an old friend. I smooth out the strap and hang it around my neck as I open the door.

Vic offers a little wave. "Remember, you can come back any time."

I step into the other room.

It's his old living room with the yellow couch and the black-and-white photographs on the walls. I close the darkroom door behind me. I stand there for a moment, absorbing where—and when—I am, not to mention which self I am. It's like my selves have telescoped into the center from two ends, teenager and adult, and here I am, squished together into a hybrid of both.

Vic saw only the seventeen-year-old me.

When I was actually seventeen, I expended so much energy waiting—longing—for adulthood, begging to get into that fabulous club. Now I find myself trapped in a time-warp version of my adolescence: all grown up on the inside but seventeen on the outside. Déjà vu or *Freaky Friday*?

I stare at the door to the darkroom, tempted to open it again, to go back in, to wrap Vic in the tightest hug and explain to him that we are family. I am trying to summon the words I would use when, just then, the red light flashes on.

CHAPTER FOUR

I REACH THE BOTTOM of those rickety stairs and round the corner to double-check the shop window. I study my reflection. I look like the same old thirty-four-year-old to me. But Vic saw a teenager. What's up with that?

There's definitely no more Amazon arrow. The giant camera on the plate glass is back.

And the heartbeat of 1967 pulsates in the street.

To adopt the vernacular of the time, it blows my mind: I'm on a repeat visit. During all the years since my last visit, in the moments when I actually believed this happened in the first place, I always assumed time travel to be a one-per-customer phenomenon. Yet here I am again. Me, Mari Caldwell, who dreads packing, traveling through time not once, but twice…so far. Is it possible this could be a regular occurrence? Hello, 1967, every seventeen years?

And why me?

Life with Nathan made me believe that most of life circles back to that one question. Why me? Life post-Nathan has made me realize that little good comes from being sucked into the vortex of that question. Sometimes it's better to direct your gaze outward instead of toward your own navel (though I can perfect navel-gazing into a fine art). Participating fully in the here-and-now is not my forte.

But with Jefferson Airplane blasting from a passing car, it's not so hard here in Hashbury. *"Don't you want somebody to love?"* It's not just a question. It's a demand—urgent, raw intense. *"Wouldn't you love somebody to love?"*

As I head down Haight, I feel lighter, like the past seventeen years have lifted off my body. A riot of color sweeps me along.

Clothing, murals, liquid-lettered posters. Photo chemicals still sting my nostrils, but I breathe easier as sweeter aromas waft through the air: weed and incense—patchouli and sandalwood, jasmine and cedar. Protesters chant a backbeat for the spontaneous music festival of the street—guitar and flute, harmonica and tambourine—while strains of folk and rock blend with the sonic hallucinations of psychedelia streaming from record stores and head shops. Music pours down from apartments above. I look up. A curtain of colored beads clinks in one of the windows.

Here's the Blue Unicorn. There's the Free Clinic. Across the street, a store called In Gear hypes the latest styles: velvet hip-huggers and bellbottom jeans. Even so, a lot of the neighborhood hasn't caught up with itself. Plenty of ordinary businesses line Haight: auto supply and electrical shops, a paint store, a dry goods store—all the merchandise no one leaves home to buy in 2024.

I find myself back at the diner again. It's right there on the window: Pall Mall Lounge. The old sign is there: twenty-five cent Love Burger. I cup my hands around my eyes to peer in, looking for the counter boy I remember, a kid not more than nine or ten years old flipping burgers on the flattop.

A few blocks down, next to a TV repair shop, I come upon the coffee house where Jimmy and the guys had that disastrous gig that temporarily broke up the band. I open the door. Years of cigarette smoke cling to every surface, while countless spilled beers have left a skudge on the floor.

The guy who runs the place sidesteps a couple of cardboard boxes as he wanders into the darkness from the even darker recesses at the back of the club.

"Frizzie?" I say. His name tumbles right out as though I just talked to him yesterday.

"Who wants to know?"

"It's me." I step into a small patch of light cast through the single window. "Mari."

"Oh sure," he says. "Long time, no see. Where you been?"

"Oh, you know…here and there. Mostly there, now back here. Unexpectedly."

"Looking for Jimmy?" he asks. He steps behind the bar and pours himself a cup of sludge from the bottom of the pot of yesterday's coffee.

Of course I am. I came looking for what was left of Jimmy, the essence of Jimmy, a memory. But now that I'm here—whoa!—I can look for Jimmy for real.

"Yes!" I say, a little too amped. "Do you know where he is?"

"Mister Big Shot rock star?" he says, nodding toward a poster on the wall over the bar. Jimmy's face—*that face*—beneath fluid, swirling letters: Neon Dream.

"Probably at the house getting ready for the thing."

"The thing?"

"You know…" Frizzie turns on the lights, scrunching his face against the brightness. He nods toward my camera hanging around my neck. "You here to shoot the party?"

"Party?"

"For the record."

"The record?"

"No radio the last two months?"

Um, Sirius XM, Apple CarPlay, Google Play, YouTube Music, Amazon Music, Spotify. Yup, I have radio. Sort of.

He continues. "They play it all the time. Big hit. I'm happy for the boys."

"And they're having a party? Today?"

"Yup," he says. "At the old homestead."

"The Victorian?"

"Yeah, you're back just in time."

"I am," I say. "In the nick of time."

—

I NEED A MAP to guide me to the old Victorian. Oops—not the map on my phone. I remember from last time: anachronisms are my natural enemy. At the very least, I should be able to spot Jimmy's van parked out front. It will be the one painted like a psychedelic Easter egg.

As I head in what I think is the direction of the band's house, I pass more than one van painted with swirling corkscrews, geometric patterns, optical illusions. It was my idea to use the leftover paint we'd used on the house—a rainbow of colors—to spruce up the old van. I guess it was the first in the neighborhood. Me—a trendsetter?

I make my way down Haight, scanning right and left at every cross street, looking for the house. Will I know it when I see it? If I see it? I think I spot it and head down Clayton, moving faster and faster, but I when I get there, it's not the one.

By the time I'm back on Haight, a ragtag parade is moving toward me down the road. Hippies making their way toward the park *en masse*, probably for a Be-In or a Love-in or some other "In." A long-hair draped in a Navajo blanket leads the way. But something feels off. It's the energy. (If I'm making sense of things in terms of energetic shift, I really am in the Age of Aquarius.)

Marchers hold candles. One carries a broom flagpole with miniature American flags stuck into its bristles. A bunch of hippies hold something high over their heads. I move closer to the throng to see what it is. It's a box. A pine coffin covered in flowers. Huh? I edge my way closer through the crowd until I can make out the words scrawled across the back: "Hippie, devoted son of mass media."

Hippies (mourning themselves?) throw stuff onto the coffin as it passes. Beads and trinkets and clothing. Posters and flowers and buttons. Weed, too. Its pungent musk hangs over the street.

Are they declaring the hippie dead? I don't understand. Isn't it still 1967? I took American Studies. I'm pretty sure '67 is still peak hippie.

I merge with the procession as it passes Middle Earth Clothing.

"What's going on?" I ask the guy next to me. He wears a combat jacket—Army Surplus?—and raggedy jeans. (Sartorially, the hippie is clearly alive and well.)

"Dig it," he says. "The whole scene's been commercialized." He points at the camera around my neck.

"I just take pictures." I explain.

"Don't become the problem," he says. "The media's got to split."

"So no more hippie?" I say, trying to wrap my head around this development.

Another guy explains. "No more Madison Avenue hippie." He points to a sign in a window: Haight Is Love. "See that? Now it's more like Rip-Off Street."

Way to spoil the vibe. Just when I'd started feeling weirdly carefree, like a kid on the first day of summer vacation. Of course, it's not that I don't feel like a kid most of the time. Do I feel old at thirty-four? I do not. I feel young, inside and out. But here in '67, the gulf between the me on the inside—adult-ish—and the way I seem to appear on the outside—seventeen-ish—feels treacherous. It could be a lot to navigate.

A convertible passes by. The guy riding shotgun raises a megaphone to his mouth: "Anything you pick up on the street, take it to the clinic so you can find out what it is." The girl next to me flashes him a peace sign. Inexplicably, so do I.

Within a few blocks, I feel entirely young. Inside and out. I'm not about to let this funereal offshoot of disgruntled defeatists yuck my yum, which is an odd attitude for me to adopt since "disgruntled defeatist" is my default setting.

Suddenly, some of the "mourners" stop. They drop to the ground, kneeling at the corner of Haight and Ashbury. So that's it—a Kneel-In.

A girl with a daisy painted around her eye plays "Scarborough Fair" on the zither.

A guy takes to a soapbox. He's wearing an army jacket covered in buttons: *Hell No, We Won't Go*; *Draft Beer, Not Boys*; *Make Love, Not War*. "Tourists came to the zoo to see the captive animals and we growled fiercely behind the bars we accepted, and now we are no longer hippies and never were."

A call-and-response goes up.

"No longer hippies!"

"Never were!"

"No longer hippies!"

"Never were!"

"No longer hippies!"

"Never were!"

I don't get it. They look like hippies to me, straight from Central Casting.

I wander along with the crowd until they reach the Panhandle where the pallbearers lay the coffin on the ground and light it on fire. Flames shoot to the sky, flickering and oscillating while everyone dances around the fire in a wild ring-around-the-rosie of abandon. Inside the blaze, the front page of *The San Francisco Oracle* catches fire, the words crumbling to ash. Someone tosses in a five-dollar bill for effect.

A television reporter in coat and tie thrusts a microphone at a guy who's all bushy mustache under a floppy hat. "What's your name?"

"Bodhi."

"Explain to our viewers, Bodhi, what this is all about. Why a funeral for the hippie?"

"We're tired of being exploited," says Bodhi. "We're done being co-opted. We've got to beat the media at its own game. That's the only way to move the human race a step ahead. We've got to change the system."

I'm about to wish him luck. He's going to need it. But behind me, I hear, "Mari?"

I turn around to find Jennifer throwing her arms wide toward me. Sam and Jennifer were the ones who found me the morning after I crashed my bike and passed out in that old VW van. She's the one who insisted I come with them to the city, landing me in 1967. I've always loved her for that. It's hard not to love Jennifer. Everything about her is lovely—her wavy brown hair, her porcelain blue eyes. But it's more than that. She has a kind of glow (that, I can assure you, does not come from a TikTok makeup tutorial).

"Where have you been?" she says.

"Around…" I say as I flip my camera over my shoulder to fall into her hug. There's still something in the way: a baby. The last time I saw Jennifer she was giving birth to Tomorrow in the little office at The Fillmore. Now, she cradles her baby girl in a batik sling wrapped around her chest. I tilt my head to see the baby's face.

"She's beautiful," I say.

"I know," says Jennifer. "She's my little moonbeam."

"How's Sam?" I say.

"He's good. He comes and goes at the house." She pats Tomorrow's head. "We live with a bunch of other people in this great house. It's great. There's a bunch of us with babies. We all help each other and share everything."

I remember my morning getting Joni off to school. A little help would have been so helpful. I'm not a huge fan of roommates or even potluck for that matter, but sometimes an extra pair of hands sounds good.

She slides a pinky into her baby's mouth. Tiny Tomorrow sucks with little slurping noises that make me ache.

"You're going to the party?" she says. She does the mommy sway.

"Yeah, the party…"

"Aren't you so excited for them?" she says.

I take a beat to realize she's talking about the band and their hit song.

"Oh yeah, totally excited. Go them."

The baby whimpers.

"The song was about you, right?" says Jennifer. Her sway grows more exaggerated, like a ship when the waves begin to pitch.

"That's the song? That's the hit?" I remember the night Jimmy wrote the song. I set out to break his heart in order to ignite his creative spark. I left him.

"Jimmy says their music's going to change the world," says Jennifer.

"I know," I say. "That's what Jimmy always says." But saying "always" makes me feel like an impostor. Who am I to know what Jimmy Westwood always says or does or thinks or feels? A million years ago I dropped in on his life and disappeared a few days later.

Jennifer hugs me close, as close as we can get given there's a baby strapped between us.

"I missed you," she whispers.

"I missed you, too," I say. Tears well in my eyes because, unexpectedly, I mean it.

CHAPTER FIVE

When I was here before, the band's house, like their van, was the only one with a colorful paint job. I held the ladder for Jimmy as the guys went crazy with yellow, chartreuse, and violet. They mixed two colors to get the lime green they used for the trim, the scrollwork, and the molding.

Today, the block of Victorians looks like a child's watercolor set, the narrow houses crowded wall-to-wall like little paints in their pans.

When I spot a lime green door, I know it's Jimmy's. Through the bay window I see a mashup of twenty-and-thirty-somethings inside. Neighborhood hippies, random locals, men in suits. The door's wide open, but I hang back. After all, I haven't officially been invited, and even if this is an open house, there's a fine line between friend-of-a-friend and party crasher. Besides, I'm suddenly not sure I'm ready to see Jimmy. I've been on a quest all day, but now that my goal is so close, my palms go sweaty and my mouth goes dry as if I were back driving across the bridge.

Jennifer rests her hand on my back, nudging gently. Her baby's only four months old, but Jennifer has got the maternal thing down: *go ahead, honey, you can do this*. I grab the wrought iron railing and head up the steps to the porch. I wait a minute. Then I go in.

I'm surprised I remember the house so vividly. But I do. Outside, every curlicue of gingerbread. Inside, every gilt flower on the crown molding; the hefty, carved banister of the staircase; the yin-yang tapestry in the stairwell; the landing's stained-glass window with its two swans, necks entwined to form the shape of a heart. Nothing has changed. Why would it? People don't redecorate every four months.

My main memory of the guys: them lollygagging in the parlor, draped across the sofa, searching for their groove. Not today. No familiar faces though the room is packed.

A navy blazer type chats up a much younger hippie chick with practiced cool. "We're hoping to get their follow-up out in a hurry," he says.

"You know what they say," she says, fiddling with an enormous hoop earring.

"What?"

"I thought you knew."

Jennifer deposits herself on an overstuffed chair. She lifts her Mexican peasant blouse and settles the baby on her massive breast. She closes her eyes like a Madonna, leaving me to do the single mingle as Sarah says. The guys from the band are nowhere to be seen. Can it be a party for their record without them? Is there no Jimmy in the house?

I navigate through the partiers toward the kitchen. It's just as crowded as the parlor, maybe more. I dig through a tub of ice for a La Croix but settle for a Tab. I pop the top and continue through to the backyard, striving for inconspicuous. I normally make myself invisible by taking pictures, but I don't want to seem like I've been hired to cover the event because: a) I'm not really sure what the event is, and b) I have no idea who anyone is and whether they'd be happy to have their picture taken or are one shutter-click away from punching out the paparazzi, which would be me.

Out back, a gaggle of folks smoke weed under a giant tree. On the other side of the narrow yard are a long, rough-hewn table and a few chairs in the shadow of a tall hedge that separates this yard from the neighbor's.

"Hello, Sunshine."

I know that voice—pure smoke and rasp. Royce. He sidles up behind me. "Where you been?" Only Royce could make that question sound lewd.

"Here and there," I say. "Mostly there."

"I thought we'd seen the last of you."

"No, it's still the beginning of me. Or at least the middle."

He cocks his head, peers at me from under hooded lids. It's a look that says he thinks there's something different about me. My cue to pre-empt further questioning.

"And you?" I say. "What's up with you?"

"Since you disappeared into thin air?" He blows on his fingers—poof. His full lips stay puckered a moment longer than is necessary. I remember now—everything he does is designed for maximum disarming quotient…and seduction. Including his tight black leather pants.

"You should've stuck around," he growls. "It's been a time around here."

"Yeah…well…it's been a lot of time a lot of places."

He takes a step closer and flicks my hair behind my shoulder.

"Do not do that," I bark. It takes him by surprise. He relies on rizz. But I'm not seventeen anymore. Except I am. To him and everyone else.

"Whoa!" he says, raising his hands outward—nothing up his sleeve. But I remember this guy. There's always something up his sleeve.

I change tacks. "So whatever happened to you?"

He furrows his brow. Whoops—weird past tense.

"I'm still happening, Sunshine," he says. "I'm managing these guys." He grabs the can of Tab out of my hand and takes a sip.

"I beg your pardon?" I say. The bad blood between Royce and Jimmy ran crazy deep.

"Sometimes you've just got to be the bigger man," he says. The picture comes into focus: since Jimmy and the guys won the Battle of the Bands, Royce just found another way to win. An easier way. He attached himself to their rising star. Jimmy's band is skyrocketing. Royce wants a piece of that. He's that guy. Attention, dollars, girls, whatever the goal—as manager of a band with a hit record, he gets it all. He wouldn't care if the girls were just using him to get close to the band. He wouldn't care one bit. "Use me," he'd say. "Use me."

"Royce. Let's get this show on the road." It's Nina. She stands in the kitchen doorway, hands on hips, flaunting her no-nonsense attitude. There's a lot of leg between the bottom of her purple velvet mini-dress and the top of her red cowboy boots. I spot her spotting me. The shift in her gaze is palpable. She inhales sharply and her eyes turn to steel. My chest squeezes.

"Where have you been?" she barks, stepping outside. No pleasantries for Nina. She's grown out her bangs. Her wild, dark mane is now parted down the middle and covers her cheeks, but her eyes are the same. Dagger-sharp. She doesn't have to say part two of her question out loud: *Where have you been and why didn't you stay there?*

"Hard to say." I try a new approach, channeling my seventeen-year-old style. The ramble. "Where have any of us been?" I say. "I don't remember much from physics, but I think some people—Einstein, likely, though Bill and Ted and their excellent adventure are possible candidates...people in general think space and time are interconnected, so it would be hard to explain where you've been without taking into account *when* you've been. Theory of Relativity, right? Which for sure is Einstein, not Bill and Ted. So...polar route answer...it all has to do with relativity. Which, actually, is the truth, I've been with relatives."

Nina rolls her eyes. Royce shakes his head. My ramble doesn't phase them. Why would it? When they knew me, it was my signature.

"So," says Nina, "Jimmy called you?" There it is.

"No, this is pure coincidence," I say. "Happenstance. Fate, if you like."

"I don't," says Nina.

"You can't argue with fate," says Royce.

Nina instructs him while staring at me. "Our boy's ready to rock. Let's go."

He rests a palm on the small of Nina's back. "Enjoy, Sunshine," he says to me as he nudges Nina toward the house. He taps the camera hanging around my neck. "All band prints get run past me."

"Groupies," he says to Nina, meant for me to hear. "They come with the territory."

"Screw the groupies," says Nina.

"Oh, I will," says Royce.

Nina jerks free of his hand and strides into the kitchen.

My shoulders drop from around my ears back to where they belong.

Royce pauses in the doorway. He turns back to the folks milling under the tree smoking dope. "It's show time, people."

I follow along into the house. The parlor is even more packed by now. Royce crosses to the staircase, climbs a few steps and turns to the crowd. "Okay, teeners, here we go. A lot of you knew this bunch of lunatics long before they were what they are. Well, Neon Dream is still a bunch of lunatics but now they've got a record the whole world's going to know. I'm thrilled to the tip of my…" (pauses lasciviously) "…boots to introduce Neon Dream! They've done what we all knew they were gonna do the first time we heard them at Frizzie's."

Frizzie stands near the front door. He pumps his fist in the air. Various fans chant, "Frizzie… Frizzie…!"

Royce and Jimmy were rivals, both aching to win the Battle of the Bands. Royce, hungry for stardom. Jimmy, to make music that would change the world. Now, Royce is spinning a story about how he always believed in Jimmy. Whatever fake narrative serves the bottom-line works for this guy. We all know the type.

One of the men in suits leans into the girl standing next to him. "I saw them there a year ago. I knew they were going to be big."

Royce continues. "Let LA have the Doors. Let LA have The Byrds. The Mamas and The Papas… Zappa… We've got the Airplane!"

Whoops spring from the crowd.

"…We've got Janis!"

More whoops. Royce conducts the crowd. His charisma is his baton.

"…We've got Neon Dream! And Neon Dream's got a hit that's zooming up the charts like a rocket."

Applause erupts.

"Let them know how much you love them!" Everyone's cheering now. I feel it too. There's a landing halfway up the staircase where it turns. Royce gestures toward it with the sweep of his arm. "On rhythm guitar. Pablo Jose Rodriguez! P.J.!"

P.J. bolts from the second floor to the landing. He's thinner than I remember—wiry, in jeans and a T-shirt. He runs a hand through his wavy black hair and does a little jig.

"The man on bass—Sam Bell." Sam, now with a scraggly reddish beard, turns toward the sound of Jennifer's whistle in the crowd. She holds baby Tomorrow high, and he makes a funny face—tongue out, eyes buggy. He tips his goofy bowler hat, then joins P.J., clapping him on the back.

"The dude who keeps the beat—Boo-Boo Abernathy." Where I come from, he's Bob and he's married to my mother. I shove that thought into the vault. Otherwise, I might spontaneously combust.

Right now, he's Boo-Boo, and Boo-Boo is not much more than a kid wearing striped engineer overalls with no shirt underneath. A lock of hair (he still has a full head) flops onto his forehead as he bounds from the second story to the landing in a single, joyful leap. It kind of breaks my heart to think of the arthritic knee waiting out there in his future. Not to mention the belly that makes him a credible Santa Claus every December. For Joni.

What's Joni doing right now? I glance at the grandfather clock in the parlor. Three thirty-five. It's unlikely any of these jokers would ever wind the thing, but if it's accurate, Nathan will have already picked her up from school. They probably stopped for ice cream on the way back to his house— *"Please, Daddy, please!"*—maybe an hour at the park, and now…I don't know what they'd be doing now. She has a life beyond me, without me. How did that happen?

Weirder still, at this moment, I'm living a life without her.

There are two band members left to introduce. Royce rests his hand on the black leather second skin encasing his muscular thigh. "There's only one chick who can keep up with this gang of miscreants…make that *put* up with them. On top of that she's got the pipes to stop your heart. On vocals and tambourine, I give you—Nina Cavendish!"

Whistles and hollers as Nina shoves her way into the clump of guys gathered on the landing, forcing Sam down a step. She would never accept anything less than center stage. She corrects Royce, "Percussion if you please."

One of the guys in a blazer—record exec, I figure—salivates at the sight of her. His eyebrows dart up as she executes a deep curtsy, extending wide the skirt of her mini-dress so that it's even mini-er.

There's one more band member to go.

This is so much more than I bargained for when I set out to find the vestiges of Jimmy Westwood. Was that just this morning?

After my first visit to '67, I considered all the explanations. Had I somehow managed to poke a finger into a miniscule slit in the time-space continuum and rip? Did my bicycle accident, that head-meet-tree whammo, jog loose a fantasy I never knew I harbored? Or the memory of a past life that might have belonged to my parents?

All theories came up short. They couldn't account for the uber intense connection I had with Jimmy. Was there some sort of intertemporal entanglement two people could share? They call it *folie a deux.* Shared madness. Literally: madness for two. Like tea. Or the tango. Maybe that's what happened to Jimmy and me.

It never occurred to me it could happen again.

"We got one more." Royce raises his hands to silence the buzzing group. "What can I say about my old pal Jimmy Westwood? We've had our moments, Jimmy and me. But you can't ignore talent like his."

Pass this guy a shovel.

"It's because of this guy that Neon Dream exists."

Actually, it's because of me. After the band bombed at Frizzie's that summer, they all quit, deserting Jimmy one by one. I'm the one who tracked them down. I'm the one who wooed each of them back, telling them, "Jimmy thinks you're the heart and soul of the band." (Hardest to say to Nina because it happened to be the truth.) So, technically, it's because of me, thank you very much.

"It's because of this guy…" Royce continues, "that we got 'Tamara Moonlight.'"

Everyone calls me Mari, so only a handful of people realize the song is for me. I'm Tamara. So, again…me. Just saying.

"He wrote it. He played it. He sang it. Here he is. Lead guitar and vocals—Jimmy Westwood!"

My limbs turn to jelly. I blink hard to focus. Am I having a stroke? I don't know if I'm wake-dreaming or dream-waking, but it's surreal.

Because there he is. There's Jimmy.

He bolts from the second floor to the landing. I can't breathe. Boo-Boo shoots him a thumbs-up. P.J. salutes him. Sam bows deeply from the waist. Nina…I don't want to look at Nina looking at him. Royce slaps him on the back, all friction between them evaporated into the intoxicating ether of a hit record.

Jimmy takes in the crowd.

I take in Jimmy. A boyish twenty-two-year-old with a slightly rugged edge, but a gentleness, too. Lean body, sloping shoulders, chestnut hair hanging loose. Those chameleon eyes—gray-green, stormy but warm. Jimmy. My Jimmy. I raise my camera to my eye and snap a photo. Click.

Someone drops the needle on a record. A warm, static crackle…an anticipatory hiss…the sound of vinyl. I get why vinyl is cool again. It's a sound charged with expectation. The gentle, melodic guitar riff comes next, then the haunting bass line, followed by the laid-back drums. It's my song.

Everyone sings along, but the volume is cranked up so that Jimmy's voice, together in harmony with Nina's, soars above them. *"Touching you, all the mysteries of life make sense to me…"*

That's the line that fills the room when Jimmy spots me. His head tilts slightly, eyes narrow, lips part. He's not sure it's me. And then he is. He smiles. That smile.

From his spot on the landing, he holds my gaze.

"Thanks for coming," he says to the crowd. "It's a trip, isn't it?" He shakes his head in disbelief. A hit record—the ultimate trip.

"Indeed, my friend," says Royce. "A trip and a half." Royce slaps him on the back again.

From the turntable, the vocals recede, leaving Jimmy's soft, melodic guitar. The last notes fade into a dream.

Someone changes the record. Suddenly, Janis Joplin is belting out, *"Love in this world is so hard to find / When you've got yours and I got mine / That's why it looks like everybody in this whole round world / Is down on me."*

Nina ushers the guys down the stairs and toward the front door. "We're outta here," she says.

"But the party's just getting good," says Boo-Boo.

"We're on a schedule," snaps Nina.

P.J. salutes her like the sergeant she is.

Jimmy pauses on his way downstairs and whispers into Royce's ear. Royce nods conspiratorially. Then Jimmy continues down with the rest of the guys and crosses to the front door.

I want to go after him but am glued to my spot, crunched in the crowd. I can feel the blood rushing through my veins. I close my eyes to let my body recalibrate. I'm metabolizing this new reality that once again includes Jimmy Westwood.

When I open my eyes, Royce stands in front of me.

"Come on, Sunshine," he says.

"I don't think so," I say.

"Just come with me."

"I'm not going anywhere with you," I insist.

"Fine," he says. "I'll tell Jimmy…"

"What about Jimmy?" I say.

"Never mind," says Royce. He loves a chance to play it cool. Nauseating. "Jimmy told me to find you…"

"Oh," I say. "Okay." I myself have never cultivated cool, but I do my stupid best.

We snake through the partiers. Out front, the crowd is less dense, but I don't see Jimmy. Royce leads me to the curb where a stretch limo waits. A hand shoots out of the back of the car, grabs my arm and pulls me in. It's Jimmy's. The rest of the band is in there too, including Nina. But all I can feel is Jimmy pulling me down onto the patch of seat next to him.

"I know, I know," I say to him. "Where have I been?"

"I don't care where you've been," he says. "I care that you're here now." He looks into my eyes. "I tried to find you," he whispers. "I wanted you here today."

"I'm here." It's hard not to kiss him. A real effort.

"You had to be here."

"I'm here," I say again, convincing myself.

Royce slides in between Nina and P.J. "Listen up," he says. "You know where this limo's taking us?"

"To the Fairmont?" says Sam.

Royce shakes his head. "To the big time, my man. To the big time."

P.J. nods. "Far out!"

Royce taps the glass partition behind him and the limo pulls away from the curb.

Sam hums "Down On Me." Everyone else falls silent, in their own heads, making sense of everything that today means.

Me, too. I look out the window to distract myself from the feel of Jimmy's thigh pressing against mine.

Turning onto Haight, we pass the Psychedelic Shop, its hand-painted sign dangling from one corner, its front window displaying chaotic heaps of merchandise. Hippies and used-to-be-hippies hang around out front snatching whatever's being given away—buttons and posters, underground comics and Zig-Zag papers. I raise the Leica to my eye and snap a photo from the backseat of the limo. Click.

Farther down Haight, murals feature mandalas, lotus flowers, and yin-yang symbols. Posters promoting concerts and love-ins. Click. Click. Click.

To be out in the world snapping pictures willy-nilly makes me feel like I've slipped back into my own skin. I look around. It feels like the city has slipped back into its own skin, too. It feels like I belong here. Especially when Jimmy rests his hand on my knee.

P.J.'s on a rant. Something about the Pentagon. I'm not paying attention. Jimmy's hand is on my knee.

We cruise along Divisadero and turn onto Geary, heading for Nob Hill. In the distance, ships are docked at the Embarcadero. Out the opposite window, the ocean shimmers under the Golden Gate, the hills of Marin visible beyond.

Marin. My so-called real life seems more distant than those ships or those hills. Today is one of those rare San Francisco afternoons when you can see forever. My real life feels that far away, forever away. I lower my head to Jimmy's shoulder. That feels pretty real.

"A blank check, I tell you," says P.J. "The Gulf of Tonkin Resolution gave LBJ a blank check."

"Old news," Sam remarks.

"But still…" says P.J. "A joint friggin' resolution."

"Speaking of joints…," Sam nods toward Royce who reaches into the pocket of his suede jacket and pulls out two joints. He hands one to Sam and one to Boo-Boo. A minute later the limo is filled with smoke.

Boo-Boo passes his to Nina. She holds it up, shaking it in their faces. "I don't want this making anyone stupid. Or silly. We've got to take this press thing seriously." Then she takes a long hit, breathing in deeply.

Boo-Boo raises his eyebrows at her.

"Nothing makes me stupid," she says. "And fuckin' nothing makes me silly." She takes another hit before passing it to Jimmy. He takes a hit and passes it to me. I hold the joint for a moment, considering. This was never my thing. Not that I had a thing, substance-wise. Not me. I pass the joint on to Sam but am suddenly compelled to explain myself like a dork in middle school.

"Asthma," I say. "I've basically outgrown it, but why take a chance? For one thing, I don't have my inhalers with me, and it seems like you guys have got somewhere important to be, so I wouldn't want to cause an ER detour because I'm all…" I clutch my chest and mime gasping for air. The limo is thick with the haze of weed. "But don't worry about all this secondhand smoke. I'll be okay. I just don't want to tempt fate…"

"Secondhand smoke?" says Boo-Boo.

"Yeah," I say, "you know…" I swirl my hand through the air.

Boo-Boo shrugs. He doesn't know.

Jimmy whispers in my ear. "I missed you," he says. "I didn't know how much."

You've got to love someone who finds your most annoying habit—in my case, my propensity for an Olympic-level ramble—to be the most charming thing about you.

P.J. flashes Royce a look. Royce digs a baggie out of his pocket, opens it wide. Inside, a mad tea party of pills. P.J. fishes out a brown capsule. Royce grabs a bottle of Jack Daniels from the built-in bar and passes it to P.J. He swigs down the pill. And keeps swigging.

Nob Hill rises in front of us. The streets are cleaner in this part of town, the houses more grandiose, the atmosphere more polished. The ride from the Haight to "Snob Hill" is a veritable essay question, so much to compare and contrast. Ultimately: less funk, more money. Entirely different ecosystems.

The limo climbs California Street. We pass the first of a string of posh hotels. We turn left on Mason and swing into the *porte cochere* of the Fairmont. (My mom would tell you that "*porte cochere*" is one of those words that tacks an extra 25K onto the price of a house.) Unlike the Victorians in the Haight, which are mostly made of wood, this place is solid. Seated on the top of the hill, its stone and brick exterior commands attention. No big bad wolf is blowing this place down.

Nina steps out of the limo. The guys tumble out after, a motley crew. I hang back as they head in. Royce looks me in the eye. "See you later, Sunshine."

Jimmy grabs my hand. "You're coming."

"Listen…Westwood…" says Royce. Jimmy shuts him up with a look.

As soon as we step inside, three men in suits converge on Royce and the band, extending their hands. It's so weird how suit guys are part of the band's scene now.

One of the suits explains to the band, "We're in the Vanderbilt. It's got a nice intimate feel."

He leads us through the lobby (like I'm part of the "us") and throws open the door with great élan. It's a smaller ballroom as ballrooms go, but has the high ceilings, gilt mirrors and rococo detail of a jewel box. It hardly feels like the kind of place a rock group would hold a press conference, but about twenty reporters wait inside.

Royce leads the band to the dais where they take their seats behind a long table like kids at a spelling bee. I stand against the wall at the back of the room, raise my camera to my eye. Click.

The exec who had his eye on Nina back at the house takes a spot near me. Late twenties, tortoiseshell glasses, hair flipping at his collar. Looks like he's trying to split the difference between mainstream and counterculture. We exchange smiles.

"Steven Blum," he says. He almost extends his hand, but thinks better of it because, after all, I'm just a kid. A handshake feels too formal. Not cool. First—and likely last—time I've ever been considered an arbiter of cool. "A&R," he adds.

Accounts and Receivable? Acquisitions and Retention? Aliens and Robots?

"Artists and Repertoire," he says. "I'm with the label."

"Mari Caldwell," I say. *Time-traveler and muse.*

The band fiddles with the microphones lined up on the table in front of them, tapping them and adjusting their angles. I smile at the A & R guy and go back to taking pictures. Mostly of Jimmy. He sits between Boo-Boo and Sam, but every few minutes, he glances at me and smiles. It's like he wants to make sure I'm here or if he imagined me. Of course, I could be projecting. I myself am wondering if I'm really here or if I imagined him.

Royce leans into P.J.'s microphone and performs a rerun of his band introductions.

Hands shoot up. Naturally, Royce calls on a girl who looks young enough to be writing for her high school paper. I guess that's the way I look, too.

"How long have you been together?" she asks. She flips open a spiral-bound steno pad.

Jimmy pulls the mic closer. "A little over a year. Off and on."

"A lot of off," P.J. fires. "Some on. Are there any other options? Off *and* on? Like the Dream's a light switch? There must be other options, man. Over, under, sideways, down…?" His hands flail wildly, illustrating what strikes him as the extraordinary concept of direction. He knocks over the mic. I don't know much about drugs, especially the sixties variety, but I'm guessing that little brown capsule was some sort of upper. P.J.'s mouth can't stop. Who does he think he is? Me?

Nina cuts him off. "Some of us have been together longer than a year." She doesn't look at Jimmy, but she might as well.

A hippie raises his hand. "*Berkeley Barb*. Don't you have an obligation to write more socially relevant songs?"

Boo-Boo shakes his head. "A great song is a great song, man."

"It's a love song," says Sam. "Love's always relevant."

Nina jumps in. "They're both right."

"You wrote it, Jimmy," says the Barb. "What do you think?"

Jimmy closes his eyes for a moment. Then he leans into the mic. "Love is universal. If you can express what someone is feeling… someone longing for love or deep in love or suffering through a lost love, then you're bringing people together. Change isn't only political. It's powerful stuff to put people in touch with their hearts. Then maybe you can change the world…" He looks right at me.

The high school paper girl turns around to see who he's looking at. I might see a flash of envy.

"Maybe you can change the world," he repeats, "one heart at a time."

That's exactly what he said to me when I asked him, all that time ago, if he really believed music could change the world. "One heart at a time." He said it then and he says it now. He smiles to see me smile.

Royce nods at another reporter, an older man with a rumpled shirt and a baseball cap. The slump of the guy's shoulders says he's seen it all, but sure never expected to be on this beat. "Mitch Sekulovich, *The Guardian*. Can you tell us what inspired 'Tamara Moonlight?'"

"Writing a song…it's kind of a magical thing," Jimmy says. "I don't like to look directly into that light. I'm kind of superstitious. Don't want to mess with that mojo. You just grab it when it comes."

Berkeley Barb pipes up. "Tamara's just a name?"

"A beautiful name," says Jimmy. "Very musical. Beautiful."

"So she's nobody special, your inspiration?"

I hold my breath. I glance at my A & R friend to make sure he can't hear my heart pounding.

Nina, who's been leaning back in her chair, pushes herself forward to the table. She leans into her mic. "Jimmy's inspiration is heartbreak. He wallows in it."

"So there's no Tamara?"

Royce chortles lasciviously. "Oh, there are plenty of Tamaras, am I right?"

Jimmy shakes his head. Nina gives him major side-eye.

"There was a Tamara when I wrote the song," says Jimmy. He takes a deep breath but doesn't look at me. "There is a Tamara." He smiles slightly. "There is most definitely a Tamara."

"Make no mistake," says Royce. "Jimmy's a free agent." Straight from the smarmy manager manual.

Nina leans back in her chair again, removing herself from this charade. But her lips purse and her jaw tightens. She's still got a thing for Jimmy.

Sam glances between Jimmy and Nina, Nina and Jimmy... Jimmy and me. The last thing Sam wants to do is blow this shot at the big time over a dumb love triangle.

"'Nuff said," says Sam.

I snap Sam's photo. Click.

More hands shoot up. What was the recording process like? Are they planning to tour? When will they be releasing the album?

The guys volley answers. Boo-Boo's having fun, I can tell. P.J. can't stop blinking, his feet tapping nonstop under the table. Sam looks eager to get out of there. Nina keeps eyes on them all. Jimmy is smiling at me, like he doesn't care who notices.

Finally, Royce raises both hands. "That's all, folks. Gotta split, but this was just the first of many."

The reporters gather their stuff as Royce tries to usher the guys and Nina out of the room.

A couple of the young reporters—both girls—corner the band. One has her pencil poised over a pad, the other holds a microphone attached to a cassette recorder. They giggle and sidle up to the guys, especially Jimmy. One of them touches P.J.'s arm. The other takes Sam's hand and writes something on his palm.

My A&R buddy turns to me. "The label thinks Jimmy's got real star quality. What do you think?" Why would he care what I think? Then I remember: I'm his target demographic.

"I think they're a great band."

"You're a diplomat," he says.

I smile and head out with the rest of the press. I feel like I am supposed to feel—how I thought I would feel when I was a grown-up—like a rock photographer on the job.

I pass through the lobby, all gleaming marble and twinkling crystal chandeliers. Gold everything. The more-is-more school of decorating. A massive clock, Roman numerals embossed against a mahogany background, reminds me that time is passing even though this place feels freakishly timeless.

I spot the limo as soon as I step outside. Nina intercepts. "Hey, Royce, I need some bread!" she calls as she hustles me into the back seat of a taxi. Royce is right there, hands over a wad of cash. She shoves a couple of bills at the driver.

She leans into the window and glares at me. "Your timing sucks. We've got business to take care of."

"I didn't mean to…" I stammer.

"I don't care what you meant," she says. "You showed up. Now un-show up. Go back to your parents. Or your boarding school or wherever. Just go back to where you came from." She nods at the driver and he pulls away.

CHAPTER SIX

I HAVE NOWHERE TO go…nowhere *else* to go. Other than the Victorian. If I go back to Vic's, I could find the now or the not now…a.k.a. another time. If Vic's darkroom is some sort of portal, I'm not ready to go there. I'm not ready to go back, by which I mean, go forward.

I direct the cabbie to the Victorian. Screw Nina. She's not the boss of me.

The party has mellowed out—the crush of partiers less dense, the decibel level down several notches. Several joints pass around—too many to count. I make my way into the dining room. Most of the platters are empty, but I grab a square of carrot cake from what's left on a tray.

A guy on the other side of the table is handing out drugs like they're part of the buffet. He nods in my direction. "Shrooms?" he asks.

"No thanks," I say. "But I know why you brought them to the party."

He stares at me.

"'Cause mushrooms are fun guys." I kill with the kindergarten set.

"Heavy," he says, nodding.

I spot Jennifer in the parlor, Tomorrow strapped to her chest. She sits at one end of the couch chatting with several girls. The girl at the other end is stretched out, her bare feet resting on Jennifer's lap. The girl's sun-kissed hair flows past her waist. Her jade eyes project just enough savvy and just enough zen. She's the Vanessa of the group, their queen bee. Every group of girls has one.

Jennifer beckons me to join them. "This is Mari," she says. "She's a beautiful person." She says things like that and means them. "How'd it go? The press thing?"

"It was good," I say. "They were sufficiently charming."

"Who wouldn't fall in love with Jimmy?" says a girl sitting on the floor in a full lotus.

Jade Eyes smiles at her condescendingly—like how lotus girl has fallen for Jimmy is so cute, while she herself has the inside track. I wonder if that's Jimmy's gift—to make each and every girl fall in love with him in a way that makes her feel like no other girl ever has or ever will. He made me feel that way.

Now, since I've been back, I've been in his company a total of an hour—maybe—and he's made me feel that way again. I wonder if Jade Eyes can see it in me.

"Someone asked when their album's coming out," I say.

Jennifer shrugs. "They're working on it. I think? Jimmy's gotta write some songs."

I nod.

Jade Eyes rises from the sofa like Venus from the sea. "He needs to be inspired," she says and floats off.

Jennifer pats the empty cushion. "Come sit with me, Mari." She smoothes the baby's downy hair. "Tomorrow wants you to."

"Thank you, Tomorrow," I say, joining them on the couch. It's the same tufted maroon velvet number where I spent the day helping Jimmy audition prospective band members after the guys bailed…before I wrangled them all back. Even though it's old and tattered, it couldn't be more comfortable. I had no idea I was so tired. I slip my camera off my neck, rest my head on the arm of the couch, and curl up.

———

I can't remember the last time I had a Jimmy Westwood dream, but I'm having one now. I must be in hyper-REM because it's one of those multi-sensorial dreams where everything is so vivid you're pretty sure you must be awake even though you know you're not. One of those dreams that has multiple wakings-up built in.

I smell clove and musk and sweat—an olfactory combo that would normally be something of an ugh, but it's Jimmy's smell so it's delicious. I hear him say my name. Like music. I feel myself smile. His face swims in front of me. I reach a hand to touch that face. I feel his hair. My eyes open.

Not a dream. This is real.

"Jimmy?"

"Yours truly," he says. The sun streaks through the stained-glass panel at the top of the window, casting a rainbow across his face. "Did you sleep here all night? On the couch?"

I look around, remembering where I am. "I guess so."

"I'm sorry," he says. He brushes my hair away from where it's stuck to my face with drool. Gross. He doesn't seem to care. "The Airplane were having a party in a suite at the hotel and Royce got us in. I got into a whole thing with Marty about maybe writing some songs together and we ended up crashing there. I sent Royce down to find you, but he couldn't."

"I left." I was long gone, as if Royce didn't know.

"It was pretty wild," says Jimmy. He kisses my forehead, the side of my eye. "Yesterday."

"Wild," I say, rubbing the kink in my neck.

"I'm sorry you didn't stay." He edges my hand away and takes over the rubbing. Electric and calming all at once—how does he do that? "Let me make it up to you."

"You don't have to…"

"I want to," he says. "I'm starving. Let's grab some French toast at Mama's. What do you say?"

I uncurl my body and sit up. "I say, I love French toast."

I make a pit stop in the tiny powder room. An oval mirror hangs over the pedestal sink from a brass-linked chain. The glass is foggy and splotched with dark patches, antiqued the old-fashioned way— by the actual passage of time. I stare at my reflection. Everyone else is seeing the old—young—me. The seventeen-year-old me.

But I honestly can't tell which vintage me I see. My recent gray hairs (utterly insulting) don't show. The circles under my eyes are less dark, less deep. I run my index finger between my eyebrows, hunting for the groove etched there. I can feel it. But I can't see it. Maybe the faintest trace? Maybe not.

I dig in the front pocket of my jeans for a lip balm but find only the stray beads from the broken string. I wash my hands with a well-worn sliver of soap, but there's no towel, so I open the cupboard in the corner of the room to hunt for paper towel…and because…who doesn't snoop in a bathroom? No towel of any kind. Just cleaning products: unopened Ajax, an aerosol can of Windex, a package of sponges sealed in cellophane. And a note from the landlord from who-knows-when: "To get you started." As if this gang were going to clean.

I wipe my hands on the butt of my jeans. There's my phone, right there where it normally lives, along with my car key fob, snug in my back pocket. This is the longest I've gone without looking at my phone in…probably forever. I slide it out and stare at the black screen. Useless. Who cares? Not me. I'm about to shove it back into my pocket, but it occurs to me I don't need it anymore. I don't want it.

I rummage in the cupboard. Behind the Windex, I find a box of S.O.S steel wool scouring pads. Unopened of course. I don't really know what steel wool is, but I open the box and slide my phone behind the scratchy little squares inside. Then I tuck the box behind the other supplies and close the cupboard. I'm not sure why I stash my phone there. For safe-keeping or for forgetting…or both.

When I open the bathroom door, Jimmy is waiting. He takes my hand and leads me through the foyer toward the front door. I dash into the parlor to pick up my camera where I left it on the couch and slip it over my neck.

"You should do that," I say.

"Do what?"

"Write songs with that guy. That group's a big deal, right?"

"*Surrealistic Pillow*?" he says.

"I beg your pardon."

"The Airplane album?"

"Right, of course," I say. "You should work with him."

"You think?"

"You don't have to be a singer-slash-songwriter… Maybe you can be a singer *and* a songwriter."

"Like write for other people?" he asks.

"Why not?"

"Maybe," he says. It's hard for him to picture. Right now, he's a heartbeat away from being an actual rock star. And being a rock star is…literally…like being a rock star.

The van is parked out front, its psychedelic paint job in full bloom. I remember painting it, swirling paisleys and amoebas across its side, turning rust spots into flowers and dents into chevrons. That day plays in my mind as though it were filmed under a strobe light, all of us running around herky-jerky, splattering as much paint on each other as on the van. I remember before we painted it, too. When it was a faded robin's egg blue. It was the magic bus that transported me from Marin across the bridge after, as Sam put it, my "bad scene with a bike and a tree." Not to mention when Jimmy taught me to drive in this thing, his hand on top of mine on the stick shift. His hand like that for the longest time before he leaned over and kissed me. We have history, this van and I.

Before we even get to the van, the rest of the guys explode out of the house.

"Where we headed?" asks P.J.

Boo-Boo's already rounding the front of the van to the driver's seat. He slides behind the wheel as P.J. climbs into the rear.

I take a step back toward the house. "You guys go." Far be it from me to be a third wheel. Make that a fifth wheel. Whatever. The day I imagined didn't have this many wheels. Besides, one of these wheels is not like the others. I don't belong. These guys bounce through their day like a pinball springing this-way-then-that. Spontaneity? Not my forte.

"You gotta come with!" says P.J.

I take another step in the direction of the house. "You could use this time to collab."

"Collaborate?" says Sam. "Us? Nah, we just wait for the boy genius." He rolls his eyes at Jimmy and climbs in next to P.J.

Jimmy looks at me. "Please come." He flashes that smile that makes it really hard not to melt. "Mama's has the best French toast."

Alright, I'm melted. Even so, this is not the brunch I pictured. I hesitate, frozen between climbing the five steps back to the porch into the house or taking the five steps to the van.

"Go with the flow," says Jimmy.

He said that to me once before. We were in the pulsing center of a Be-In in the park surrounded by half-naked bodies—vibing, undulating, uninhibited. All the things that are non-me. Surprise, surprise…I reacted with snark.

"You could try being a little more open-minded," he said that day.

"You can be so open-minded your brains fall out," I countered. Not my best comeback.

Jimmy didn't care. "Sometimes you've just got to go with the flow."

"I don't do flow," I said. "Flow is highly overrated."

I've thought of that moment many times. I think of it now. And of how Jimmy, refusing to let me get away with anything, said simply, "But you never know where it will take you." And then he smiled.

Like he's smiling now.

I step up into the passenger seat. In the back, P.J. and Sam slide over so Jimmy can squeeze in next to them.

Oh well. But at least I don't look like the girl who gets all pouty because a bunch of her boyfriend's friends are coming along when she thought she was going to be alone with him. Boyfriend?

(There should be a better word for the guy to whom you ceded your virginity, no matter how long ago.) At least there's no Nina. Grateful for small favors.

Boo-Boo zigzags to Van Ness. "I'm doing Eggs Benedict," he says.

I fight the urge to tell him he's going to have high cholesterol. "Maybe pancakes," he considers. "Maybe both." Bring on the Lipitor.

P.J.'s mind is elsewhere. "Pentagon exorcism, what do you think?"

"Album title?" Sam wonders.

"No, for real," says P.J. "Might be the only way to penetrate the military industrial complex."

We stop at a red light on Powell. Next to us, a cable car clanks down the street in the opposite direction. I twist around to lock eyes with Jimmy, raise my eyebrows and give the slightest nod. Jimmy hops out of the van and throws open my door. He grabs my hand. We leap out and he slams the door.

"Catch you on the flip side!" he waves to the guys. We take off across the street and propel ourselves onto the cable car. It's sort of a Bonnie and Clyde moment, without the guns.

We perch on the outer ledge of the cable car, clinging to the pole, Jimmy behind me, his arms around mine. I grin at him over my shoulder and we both start laughing for no good reason, except every good reason, including the biggest good reason—we're young (in a manner of speaking) and, dare I say, in love.

We clang-clang-clang our way through the city. The rumble of the workings underground vibrates through me, the heartbeat throb of the city matching my own.

We hop off at Columbus. Hand in hand, we wander North Beach past murals and graffiti, the twin peaks of a cathedral rising above the neighborhood. The sign for the Condor Club looms over us with its giant caricature of a blonde in a bikini. The Hungry I promises "Totally Topless College Coeds." It's massively un-PC, but, ironically, there's an innocence to the whole scene. Hard to explain.

We duck into an Italian deli where Jimmy buys a sub to share—multiple varieties of salami, paper thin provolone cheese, mortadella studded with little discs of fat. Ordinarily, I wouldn't be caught dead eating that stuff. (Insert punchline.) But right now, I don't care. This sandwich is delicious…and, including a bag of chips, costs seventy-five cents. Seventy-five cents. Like if you had a few minutes, you could pay for the whole thing in actual pennies.

Jimmy watches me dig in as we head down Columbus. He swipes a glop of mayo from the corner of my mouth with his finger and smiles like something's funny.

"What?" I say. I'm talking with my mouth full. Who cares? Not Jimmy. Not me.

"Nothing."

"No," I coax, "tell me."

"It's just that Nina won't eat this kind of thing. She says it's full of chemicals. She's bonkers."

Oh. Nina. And nitrates and sodium and preservatives, oh my.

I hate it when she's right, let alone prescient. But I love that he loves me loving this sandwich. I take another bite. A giant one, partly because it's so yummy, partly out of spite toward Nina.

I look up to see Royce drive by in his top-down Mustang, black and shiny like his leather pants. He drives with one hand, elbow propped against the open window, the other arm stretched across the back of the passenger seat…where Nina sits. They stop at a light a half-block up. I can't hear, but she's laying into him about something or another rapid-fire.

We're coming up on City Lights Bookstore. "Let's pop in here," I say to Jimmy before he can spot them.

Inside, the smell of dust and aging paper hangs in the narrow aisles. Overstuffed shelves reach from floor to ceiling. In the front room, the New Release table is piled high with copies of *The Outsiders*. I never read the book but I saw the movie. I think it's a Broadway show now. A movie of the musical can't be far behind.

We head upstairs. At City Lights, it's basically mandatory to pay homage to the beat section—Kerouac, Ferlinghetti, Ginsberg.

"You gotta read these guys," says Jimmy. He talks about them reverentially, like they're icons of a hip, cool time long gone. A whopping ten years.

We move on to the small section of records in the back room. I rifle through. Cream—*Disraeli Gears*; The Beach Boys—*Smiley Smile*; The Moody Blues—*Days of Future Passed*.

"Pretty soon, we'll be in here," he says. "Neon Dream."

I pull a Buffalo Springfield album from the stack. A couple songs look vaguely familiar, but I couldn't sing them. "When's your album coming out?" I ask.

"As soon as I finish writing the songs," he says. "And then recording them. Three, four months, I think."

I glance at the names of the guys in Buffalo Springfield. "Oh wow!" I say. "Some of these guys turned into Crosby, Stills, Nash & Young."

"You mean…" he says. "Crosby? Like David? He's in The Byrds."

"Oh right. I mixed them up." No, actually, they mixed themselves up…into a supergroup. "How do you have a hit record if your album's not…an album yet?"

"The single's a hit," he says. "Blows your mind, huh?"

"It's unbelievable."

"I couldn't have done it without you." He picks up a copy of *Are You Experienced*. "Hendrix," he says.

"'Nuff said," I say.

Jimmy laughs at my co-opting Sam's catch phrase. He ruffles my hair like aren't I just so adorable, speaking the band's native language and all.

I approach the clerk unloading a box of books onto a display table. "Where would we find the singles?" I ask.

He pushes his wire-rimmed glasses up on his nose. "Sorry, we don't carry forty-fives." He goes back to stacking the table with copies of *Rosemary's Baby*. When he bends over, his *Snoopy for President* button clanks against the side of the box.

Outside, the smell of marinara and garlic follows us down Columbus past trattoria after trattoria. The lunch crowd straggles out of the Old Spaghetti Factory as we drift toward the park.

"Let's get lost," says Jimmy, eyes wide with adventure.

"I'm a little phobic about getting lost," I confess.

"How can you be phobic about getting lost?" he wonders. Legitimately, I might add. It's a really weird fear.

"Well," I say, "there are all kinds of reasons. Separation issues, fear of abandonment, generalized anxiety disorder. I'm sure they're all factors, but it probably comes down to a control issue."

He stares at me.

"TMI?" I say. He stares at me, puzzled. Anachronistic slip of the vernacular. "Too much information," I clarify.

"Not at all," he says. He takes a beat. "It's not easy being you, is it?"

I feel my face flush, half self-conscious, half chagrined, half achingly understood —"seen" as they say. That's how Jimmy makes me feel—like an actual human by an extra half.

"I don't mean that in a bad way," he says. "Only that you've got all the words when sometimes fewer words might be better."

"Better how?"

"I don't know," he says. "Closer to the truth?"

My breath catches. I'm out of words.

We walk in silence for a while, holding hands, passing coffee houses and jazz clubs where the managers are posting notices of who's on the bill that night.

I spot a record store up ahead. It's called Hear & Now. "Let's go in. I want to see your record in the wild."

"I spent a lot of time in that store growing up," he says.

"You grew up around here?"

"Yup, I'm a Richmond kid."

"I don't know much about you, do I?" I say.

"You know everything about me," he says. "Everything that counts. Just like I know everything that counts about you."

"You do?"

"Sure," he says. "You're scared of all kinds of crazy things—bridges and getting lost—but you're the bravest person I've ever met. You ran all over town all by yourself talking the guys back into the band."

"You knew that?"

"Of course I knew that." He leads me to the back of the store where the singles are for sale. "You're like a magic trick. You appear, then you disappear. You're a quicksilver girl." He freezes, closes his eyes for a moment. "Wow," he says, "that's a song… I told you. You're magic."

We shuffle through the wacky little records, way smaller than albums. Most are in plain paper sleeves with a big cut-out so you can read the name of the song on the label. Some have pictures on the sleeve. I remember now—Neon Dream should have the picture that I took of the band.

There it is. The guys and Nina in front of the Victorian, newly painted. Boo-Boo called it that day: "Hey, man, we could get an album cover out of this." It's not an album—not yet—but it is a bona fide hit record. I slip the record out of its sleeve, hold the vinyl disc in my hands, and stare at the label. "Tamara Moonlight." Wow. That's me.

"Every week I'd get my allowance," Jimmy says. "Fifty cents. So every two weeks, I'd have a dollar to come and buy a record. Most of the time I knew what I was gonna buy, but sometimes I'd take my time. I'd spend hours looking through them." He nods toward the far end of the store. "That closet over there? With the window papered over? That used to be a little listening booth. You could go in and listen before buying. I used to drive the guy crazy, I spent so much time in there. It got so he'd see me walk in the front door and say, 'Westwood, five's your limit.' I never thought…I never dreamed…" He takes the record from me and holds it against his heart. Click.

I grab Jimmy and kiss him right there in the 45 rpm aisle. Possibly, probably, longer than I've ever kissed anyone in a public place in my life.

When I open my eyes, a little girl is staring at us agape. She's ten or eleven, dressed in a school uniform: plaid skirt, button-down shirt, knee socks riding down at the end of her school day. She's poking through the 45s.

I take the record from Jimmy and hand it to her. "You want this one," I say.

"I do?" says the girl.

"Absolutely," I say. "It'll change your life."

CHAPTER SEVEN

We meander through Golden Gate, pausing here and there to listen to the music rising out of the park every hundred yards. Guitars and harmonicas, kazoos and hand drums.

Where the grass slopes upward, there's a festival feel, though it's just another Saturday in the park, thick with people—playing music, pulsating to the groove, lying intertwined on the grass. An older man stands on the knoll singing. He looks downright professorial with his cropped gray beard, blazer, and necktie. He serenades anyone who cares to listen. *"Do what you like, do what you will / Come and join us on hippie hill / Joyous in the sun, magic in the dark / Oh hippie hill in Golden Gate Park."*

"Might as well," I say.

For a minute or two, we fall in with a line of trippies snake-dancing across the hill. We come upon one guy, shirtless in jeans and moccasins, playing "Tamara Moonlight." He bungles some of the words and stumbles over a few chords, but he's playing that song. My song. Jimmy's song. I lock eyes with Jimmy. He's got all the feels: disbelief, pride, so much joy. His joy is my joy.

We break free, cross Stanyan and head up Haight.

We pass what seems to be a co-op: Far-Fetched Foods.

"It's all health food," says Jimmy. "Everyone goes there."

"Yeah," I say, "until Whole Foods opens in the neighborhood."

"What?"

Another oops. "I mean," I say, "foods that haven't been processed. Unprocessed whole foods should be in every neighborhood."

"I guess," he says.

No point in telling him that by the time whole food becomes Whole Foods, he'll need to write a hundred smash hits to afford a head of lettuce.

The sun has dropped lower in the sky, but it's freakishly warm for a San Francisco October. I catch myself from commenting on climate change. I'd rather enjoy the warmth than consider it a global omen.

We cross to the shadier side of the street and pause in front of a store called Time & Again. The sign out front pleads: *Save The Planet—Don't Buy New!* Music pours from inside: "*I've got to admit it's getting better / A little better all the time (it can't get no worse).*"

"We gotta go in," says Jimmy. "Every time I cruise by here, I find something far out."

"Hey, Jimmy!" The clerk raises a hand in greeting. There's a lot of facial hair going on around the Haight, but this guy's got a distinctively bushy mustache.

"Hey, man," says Jimmy. "What's happenin'?"

"You know, just trying to move the human race a step ahead."

I knew I recognized that stache. He used the same line with the reporter at the Death of the Hippie Funeral.

"And doing all we can to make sure there's still a planet when we get there," he adds.

"That's heavy," says Jimmy.

"He's right," I jump in. "We're in big trouble…starting with climate change. I mean, seriously…greenhouse gases, rising tides, and extreme weather events."

Jimmy stares at me, baffled. "Extreme what?"

"Huge wildfires wiping out towns. And torrential storms. Then the mudslides. And that's just California." I'm on a roll. "Not even mentioning pollution. I know you know about pollution. The ozone layer. And plastics. And…all the industrial waste. Take it seriously…please," I try to wind down, "…man."

"Wow," says Bodhi, "you're really hip to this stuff."

"I'm no expert, just a big fan of the planet. You know, I try to use cloth napkins…no single use water bottles."

They're having a hard time making the connection. I can't back-pedal, so I go for a perky slogan. "So, you know: reduce, reuse, recycle." I gesture toward the sign outside. "Just like you said."

"I like it," nods Bodhi. "I'm Bodhi."

"I'm Mari."

"Tamara," says Jimmy.

It takes Bodhi a beat. "As in…?"

Jimmy nods. He slings an arm around my shoulder and kisses my temple. Just a sweet little peck, but a rush of heat flushes my cheeks.

"I can dig it," says Bodhi.

The table in the middle of the store is cluttered with all kinds of stuff: old board games, dog-eared paperbacks, records already vintage—Bill Haley & His Comets, Harry Belafonte, The Chordettes.

Next to the table is a rack with old clothes. I rifle through and pull out a long Indian print dress with bell sleeves, like something Jennifer would wear. Unlike anything I've ever worn or would wear.

"You can try it on over there," says Bodhi, nodding toward a curtained-off corner. I pull the curtain closed and step out of my jeans. The beads shoved deep in the front pocket rattle against each other. I yank off my sweater (oatmeal-colored crewneck—so blah) and slip the dress over my head. The fabric is crimson and gold—colors I typically eschew but feel appropriately autumnal. A different pattern in the same colors forms a bib across the chest and borders the hem. Very Olsen twins boho chic.

A mirror leans against the wall. I take a look. I kind of love it. I throw my Leica around my neck and slide back the curtain.

"There she is!" says Jimmy.

I do a little spin. The skirt flounces out around my legs. It's so much fun, I spin again. Who is this person, twirling in a crummy thrift store while her boyfriend (again—word required, please) beams?

"It's yours," says Bodhi.

"How much?" I say.

"On the house. It's meant to be yours."

"Thank you," I say. "I'll pay it forward."

"You've got the best way of putting things," says Bodhi.

I place my folded jeans and sweater on the counter. "Do you have a bag?"

"We don't do bags," says Bodhi. He takes a ball of twine from under the counter and fishes for the end. He cuts a length of string and hands it to me. I slide it under my clothes and tie it into a bow. Bodhi cuts the loose ends.

"Perfect," I say.

"Let me buy something, man," says Jimmy, digging through a Native American basket filled with beads. He pulls out a strand—some glass, some wood, some ceramic—and hands it to me. My eye goes immediately to one the size of a gumball, vividly colored and delicately filigreed.

"This is beautiful," I say.

"What do I owe you?" Jimmy asks Bodhi.

"Whatever you like."

Jimmy digs in his pocket and hands over a dollar bill.

"You're going to go out of business if you keep that up," I say, slipping the beads over my head.

Bodhi shrugs. "Just have to make it through law school."

"You're in law school?" I didn't mean to sound so shocked. No insult intended.

"Boalt," he says.

"Berkeley, right?"

He nods.

"Wow," I say, hoping I'm not insulting him again.

"We've all got to figure out the best way each of us can change the world," says Bodhi.

"One heart at a time," I say, quoting Jimmy. He smiles at me—a shared secret.

"Or one mind," says Bodhi.

"Thank you," I say, tapping the beads resting at my neck.

"Thanks, man," says Jimmy.

He grabs the bundle and we head out, me in my new dress (happily, my new *old* dress).

"Come again!"

"You never know," I say.

As the sun begins to set, we wander the neighborhood. We pass The Diggers' Free Store and another shop called Trip Without A Ticket. I sense a theme: take what you want, pay what you can. Retail free-for-all. Freetail.

"Let's take a selfie," I say.

"A what?"

"A picture of us." I position Jimmy in front of Trip's storefront window and stand at his side. I lift the Leica hanging around my neck and hold it at arm's length. Not the easiest selfie.

"Turn around," I tell Jimmy. "We need to face the window."

I wait for the hippie couple reflected in the window to pass before taking our picture. They don't move. That hippie couple smiling at each other in the window is us. Click.

We crisscross the streets of San Francisco until we end up in Chinatown. Ornate lanterns line the street. The smell of duck fat and five spice wafts through the air. Storefronts feature paper parasols and teas, exotic spices and ancient remedies, wind chimes and lucky bamboo. We veer off the main artery, Grant Avenue, and find ourselves in more of an alley than a street, lured by the smell of something toasty and sweet. It's the Golden Gate Fortune Cookie Factory.

"Fortune cookies!" I say. "Let's get some."

Jimmy pauses in front of the metal awning, blue with red pagoda trim.

"I know what my fortune is," he says. He takes my face in his hands. "I missed you, but I didn't know how much."

"Me too," I say. "I missed everything here."

"Everything?"

I nod. "Everything." I step closer to him and wrap my arms around his waist. He's lean and sinewy. He feels exactly the way you expect a rock star to feel if you were…for example…in the audience at a concert and imagined wrapping your arms around the guy on stage. Destined for rock stardom by virtue of body type? Who knows. It doesn't matter. I've known this is exactly how he feels for exactly half my life.

"Everything," I say again. I raise my face to his. He kisses me. It's the kiss version of the aroma that fills the air. Warm fortune cookies—toasty, sweet, vanilla—when the cookies are fresh out of the oven, still full of promise, their messages not yet sealed.

We wind our way through the alleys of Chinatown. There's no question where we're headed. Sam Wo's. "Chow Mein—Noodles—Soups—Fish—Salad."

We pass through the kitchen where cleavers slice the air and hot oil hisses in giant woks. We climb the same narrow, creaky flight of stairs that we did that night in June of '67.

It's just as I remember. Bare bones, zero décor, feeble lighting. None of these things make Sam Wo's what it is. Good old Edsel the waiter does that. A tall guy with a round face and a crewcut, Edsel is berating customers as we arrive in the doorway. "I be back in two minutes. You be ready!" he orders a table of diners.

Then he points at a couple ahead of us at the top of the stairs. "Sit down and shut up!" They head for a table in the corner of the cramped dining room.

He spots Jimmy. Edsel shakes his head at the other couple. "No. You wait. Table not ready."

"But…"

Edsel nods at Jimmy. "Jimmy, you come sit."

"We were here first," the guy stammers. His girlfriend places her hand on his arm to silence him.

"Who cares," says Edsel. "Jimmy here now."

The place is full. Tourists know it's not a trip to Chinatown unless they've been yelled at by Edsel.

Jimmy and I sit at the corner table. Edsel pulls up a chair and joins us. "So," he says, "you big rock star now."

"Not really…" says Jimmy.

"Don't pretend with Edsel. You got hit record. Edsel proud of you. But listen to Edsel."

"Always," says Jimmy.

"Stardom…" Edsel waves his hand through the air. "Then what?"

"I don't know," says Jimmy.

"I tell you."

A diner at the next table leans over. "We've been waiting a really long time…"

"Good things come to those who wait," says Edsel.

"Or in this case, so-so chow mein comes to those who wait," says Jimmy.

Edsel scowls at him from under his brows. "What comes after stardom?" he says. "Sometimes, most times…no more stardom."

Jimmy nods.

Edsel pauses. Then, "Just life. That's what comes. Rest of your life." He stands, prods Jimmy with a chopstick. "You think about that."

Edsel stands and gives me the once-over. "I remember you. Still with camera, but something different about you this time." Last time, I earned his stamp of approval. I don't want him to withdraw it now.

"My hair might be a little shorter?" He gives me the full Edsel glare. "Maybe a little longer? It's hard to keep track—it grows all the time, as hair does…"

Edsel shakes his head. "Not hair. Nothing to do with hair." He crosses to another table to take an order. "What you want?" he barks at the customers. "You can't order that, that dish no good—no egg foo young tonight."

Jimmy shakes his head. Edsel—what can you do? Then he smiles at me. "I remember you're someone who thinks about the rest of your life all the time."

I take the little stopper out of the soy sauce bottle, put it back in.

Across the room, Edsel yells at a diner. "No Coke! You retarded! Tea only."

"I used to…" I say. "Think about my future, I mean. All the time. I used to be obsessed."

"Yale," he says.

"Yup."

"When do you find out if you got in?"

I spill a little soy sauce on the table, mop it up with a napkin.

"I'm not sure," I say.

"Oh yes you are," he says.

"No, honestly, I've forgotten when they tell you. I mean, Yale's fine but maybe it'll turn out that it's not all it's cracked up to be."

"Are you having second thoughts about going?"

"I should have had second thoughts, but it's too late for that."

He studies me quizzically.

"I'm committed."

"You can always change your mind about what you're committed to," he says.

I feel the glib motor revving up. I could easily riff for ten minutes. When he knew me before—four months and seventeen years ago, or fifty-plus years ago depending on how you do the math—that's precisely what I would have done. Instead, I take a deep breath.

"I want to be committed to here and now," I say. "To this place and time."

"Then don't just want to be," he says. "Be committed."

"I am committed," I say. "Committed. There's no place like here. There's no place like now."

"There's no place like now," Jimmy says. "There's no place like now," he repeats. He's filing the line away for a song.

Edsel reappears, balancing a tray of dishes fresh from the dumbwaiter. He places them in front of us: wor wonton soup, barbecue pork noodle, broccoli beef. He stares at me as he ladles the soup.

"Not hair," he says, still trying to figure me out. "You older."

I hold up my hand, counting on my fingers one by one. "July… August…September…October… Four months will do that to a girl," I say.

He doesn't laugh. Of course, Edsel never laughs. He peers at me.

I stare him down. "Let's just say a lot has happened since the last time you saw me."

He isn't convinced, but he moves on to another table and snatches the menus out of the diners' hands. "You don't choose. Edsel bring you what's good."

"You want to tell me?" says Jimmy. He fishes a shrimp from the soup with a flat-bottomed spoon and pops it in his mouth.

"Tell you what?"

"About the lot that has happened?"

I consider trying the truth. I wish it weren't impossible. "Let's just say," I vamp, "it was an affair of the heart."

He nods slowly, serves us both some broccoli beef, rich with the aroma of oyster sauce and garlic. "A guy," he says.

"You might say that."

"It's over?"

I take a beat. "It is."

"When did it start?" he asks. "I guess what I want to know is, and I'm not proud of wanting to know… Did it start before you were here last time?"

"No," I say, poking at a piece of broccoli with a chopstick. "Definitely not."

"So it was just a few months?"

Trick question. I say nothing. I'm determined not to lie to Jimmy. But the truth is… Who knows what the truth is. I haven't thought about Nathan in two whole days. That's a record.

"I get it," he continues. "Short but intense."

"Something like that."

"I'm sorry if you had your heart broken."

"Things don't always turn out the way you planned."

"They rarely do," he says. He plops a dollop of hot mustard into his soup. "You did a number on me when you walked out."

I remember the night perfectly. Nina made me understand that Jimmy could only create when he was brokenhearted. He needed a song for the Battle of the Bands. So I walked out and broke his heart. It worked. He wrote our song. It sounds pretty stupid now, but it made sense at the time. Of course, we'd only been together for a weekend. Tonight, at Sam Wo's, I'm reminded that sometimes a weekend isn't just a weekend. Sometimes a weekend feels like the beginning of a whole life.

"I'm sorry," I say.

"After a couple of minutes, I came after you."

"What?"

"When you left that night."

My eyes widen.

"I couldn't find you," he says.

"I wandered around," I say. "When I passed that place where they have the Love Burgers, the little boy who worked there came out and gave me a hamburger. For free."

"I couldn't find you," he says again.

"No, I guess not," I say, conjuring what my life might have looked like if he had.

"I called your name," he says. "Really loud."

"You did?"

"Like a lunatic."

"Like Marlon Brando? 'Stella!?' Or Benjamin? 'Elaine!?'"

He looks at me askance.

"The movies," I say.

He cocks his head.

"They tend to be my reference points," I explain. "My father and I...old movies were sort of our thing when I was growing up...I mean, I'm still growing up...I guess you're always growing up, or growing anyway...we don't ever want to stop growing, right? But you know what I mean...when I was younger...you know, younger than...yesterday. Anyway, my dad and I spent a lot of time watching old movies. Especially after my parents got divorced. My weekends with him, we'd watch at least two, sometimes three or four. Once we did five—one on Friday night, one in the afternoon and one at night on Saturday and Sunday. Lots of popcorn. We got really creative with the mix-ins. Chocolate chips, caramel sauce, curry powder, bacon bits, wasabi..."

"Wasabi?"

"Yeah, wasabi." I have nowhere to go with this faux pas. Zero idea when sushi became popular. "It's Japanese," I say.

"Sounds fun," he says. "The whole movie thing."

"It was."

"There must be a lot of revival houses where you live."

Uh-oh.

"My dad was such a movie fan he actually had a projector," I adlib. "An old sixteen millimeter thing—and there was this place that rented old movies. It was a whole production, no pun intended."

"Wow," he says. "So cool."

"It was," I say. "Fathers and daughters...nothing should ever get in the middle of that," I say.

Jimmy takes a beat. "You and your dad... All good?"

I nod. "You?"

"He left when I was ten," he says.

"I'm sorry."

He shrugs. "Same old story."

"It's not the same old story when it happens to you."

Jimmy refills our teacups, peers into his as though he might read the leaves. "No, it's not," he says without looking up.

Edsel places a plate of egg foo young on our table.

"I thought there was no egg foo young," I say.

"You smart girl. Don't be stupid. No egg foo young for them," Edsel barks. "Egg foo young for you."

"Egg foo young for us," Jimmy says. He digs in.

Edsel gives me the once-over again. "Not hair," he says. "More than hair." Then he's off. We eat in silence for a minute or two. It's not even awkward.

"It's a good thing you didn't find me that night," I say. "You might not have written that song. It's a great song."

"I'm glad you like it," he says. "It's important to me that you like it. I've been hoping I'd hear from you."

Oh. He thinks I've chosen to reappear now because he's knee deep in the whole hoopla situation.

"That's not why I came back. I didn't know the song was a hit…yet. I only knew I wanted to find you." The circumstances of wanting to find him—or what I thought was going to be the essence of him—are immaterial. I *was* looking for him. I exhale with relief, having landed on the truth with no fancy verbal footwork.

"Cool," nods Jimmy.

A guy sits at the table next to us—hair to his shoulders, peace symbol around his neck. He takes out a notebook, its cover intricately decorated with tooled leatherwork. I know that notebook. I know that face at all its various ages. It's Mr. Chappell, once my high school teacher, now the *Good Morning* guy at Joni's elementary school. Here and now, he's a full-out hippie.

I raise the Leica to my eye. When I look through the viewfinder, Mr. Chappell is staring right into it. I lower the camera, chagrined. He nods at me, giving me the go-ahead, then he raises a chopstick like a baton and smiles into the lens. Click.

CHAPTER EIGHT

"Come back soon," says Edsel.

"I will," says Jimmy.

"I mean her." Edsel nods at me. Phew. Stamp of approval intact.

"I'll try," I say.

"Not so much time before next time," snaps Edsel.

"Not so much time," I repeat.

"Big shot rock star," he says, nodding toward Jimmy. "But remember… We only really rich in time."

We climb down the creaky stairs and pass through the kitchen. Outside, nighttime has softened the garishness of Chinatown. With all the neon glowing, the sharp edges of daytime are blurred. We pass the Grandview Movie Theater. Its marquee declares simply "Chinese Pictures."

"Let's go to the movies," says Jimmy.

"You speak Chinese?" I wonder.

"No," he laughs, "not this movie. Another movie. All your talk about movies…" His eyes widen. "Want to see the Dylan movie? Things have been so crazy I haven't had the chance."

"I thought it wasn't coming out till Christmas."

"Oh no," he says. "It's been out for a while."

Duh. Wrong decade, wrong Dylan movie.

"*Don't Look Back?*"

I've seen it at least three times. As far as my dad is concerned, the film demanded repeat viewings, ticking multiple boxes in my education as a human: cinematic, musical, cultural. I guess you'd have to say Bob Dylan is a box unto himself.

"Groovy!" he says. "We're going to the flicks!"

"We're going to the flicks!" I echo, just because it sounds so much fun to say.

Finding out where the movie is playing turns out to be a multi-step process. We have to find an actual newspaper which means finding an actual newspaper stand.

Two cable cars and one bus later, we make our way down the aisle of the theater just as the lights dim.

On screen, there's Bob—his face all sharp angles, his hair tousled, his gaze piercing. He stands in an alley flipping cue cards. *"Johnny's in the basement / Mixing up the medicine / I'm on the pavement / Thinking about the government…"*

The theater is packed, but we find two seats on the side up front. Jimmy is instantly riveted…and my eyes are as much on him as the screen—the rhythm of his breath, the rise and fall of his chest. The audience sings along as Dylan flips those cards, each scrawled with a word or two: *Watch It!*, *Suckcess*, *Man Whole*… When he reaches: *"You don't need a weatherman to know which way the wind blows,"* the theater erupts. You can feel it—a heady mix of rebellion and belonging, a spirit of us-against-them that is, astoundingly, more naïve than belligerent. By the time Bob flips the last card: *What??* I'm on board. Sign me up.

I watch Jimmy watching Dylan spar with a journalist from *Time* magazine.

"I got nothin' to say. These things I write…" says Dylan, "I don't write 'em for any reason."

Like a lot of the audience, Jimmy chuckles. But even in the dark, I can see bewilderment flash across his face. Sure, Dylan's putting this guy on…except, does he mean it just a little? Jimmy is filled with purpose. What is he supposed to do with all that if Dylan's just dashing off songs willy-nilly? And how do they pour out of him so easily?

Jimmy reaches over and holds my hand. A tingle shoots through me. I rest my head on his shoulder as Joan Baez's voice ricochets around the theater like a bell: *"Strange it is to be beside you / Many years the table turned / You'd probably not believe me / If I told you all I've learned..."* Jimmy kisses the top of my head. I turn my face toward him. He kisses me. I kiss him. And Joan sings: *"Love is just a four letter word."*

We make out like a couple of high schoolers. Not that I would know from personal experience since high school was not exactly the apotheosis of my romantic life, though here in this packed movie house with Bob and Joan, I feel like I might be apotheosizing right this very moment.

Jimmy's hand rests on my knee, and it's like the first time he touched me however long ago. The first everything. That night in his room in the Victorian, the chenille bedspread wadded at the foot of the bed, the rest of the world receded. Suddenly, the force field around me dissolved when I wasn't looking, like a magic trick. I'd been so focused on misdirection—don't look for me here, don't look for me there, you're never going to corner me anywhere—that I didn't even notice when Jimmy snuck in and performed the real magic. He saw me as a person who didn't need the force field anymore, who only thought she needed it all along.

—

I CAN'T WAIT TO get back to the house. It's late and we sneak in quietly. Kind of thrilling. Jade Eyes and another girl are asleep foot to foot on the sofa in the parlor.

A hushed conversation is going on in the kitchen: a guy and Nina. "He doesn't want to do a whole album of covers," she insists, her attempt at a whisper.

The guy responds. Might be the record exec guy. Probably is. Jimmy strains to hear, even though he pretends not to.

"How can I hurry him up?" says Nina. Definitely talking to the record guy.

Jimmy freezes, cocks his head toward their conversation. "No way," continues Nina. "I've been down that road."

Jimmy stares at the floor. I place two fingers under his chin and raise his face to mine. I shake my head slightly, just enough to say: *Don't mind her.*

He takes me by the hand and leads me silently upstairs to the last room on the left, his room. I remember it perfectly—the peeling plaster, the cabbage rose wallpaper, the old-timey child's school desk. It's all the same. Except for the bed. The single has been swapped out for a double. It's not all that much bigger, just bigger enough for…whatever the requirements of rock stardom. I don't want to know. The bed takes up most of the wall. But the bedspread is the same: the chenille—a sad dusty rose, pilled more than not—still bunched at the foot of the bed.

We are at each other in a heartbeat. I slip off my camera and set it on the little desk in the corner. He lifts my hippie dress over my head while I yank his shirttail out of his jeans with a single tug. He steps back for a moment, eyes wide. *Who is this girl?* He seems to like her whoever she is. (Thinking of myself in the third person is so much easier than reconciling the two first persons currently occupying me.)

We lie on the bed, limbs immediately entangled. I struggle to undo his belt, the buckle a heavy brass thing, chunky and rococo. I take this as a sign. Maybe I should stop. Maybe this is a little too creepy. I'm too young to be a cougar (major cringe), but certainly old enough to be his big sister or youngish aunt. I'm thirty-four years old. He's twenty-two. I'm something like a good one-third older than he is. No, that's not right. I'm more than half his age older than he is. Fifty-something percent. Whoa. I draw back, putting some air between us.

He kisses me. I can't stop my hand from cradling the back of his head. His hair, velvet to my fingertips, flips at the nape of his neck. He radiates the kind of heat that comes with being on the cusp—the cusp of adulthood, the cusp of success, the cusp of the rest of your life. He's so lucky.

So am I. I'm getting a do-over.

He props himself up on one elbow, his head on his hand. "The last time I saw you..." he says, "you know, over the summer...you said you had something you needed to tell me. You said you had to tell me the truth about you... Is there something I should know?"

It's now or never. Or, given what I've learned about the nature of time, is now-or-never a specious assumption? I scan the room to make sure of where I am. The dress that Jimmy just peeled off me lies puddled on the floor. My jeans and sweater, still tied with twine from the thrift store, lie where Jimmy dropped them on the floor. But here I am naked in bed with Jimmy Westwood, wearing only my locket and a strand of love beads, and it doesn't matter one bit which set of clothes I shed to be here.

"There isn't anything you need to know," I say.

"It won't make a difference. Whatever it is."

"I know," I say.

"That other guy...?"

I shake my head. "There was no other guy. Not really. I was only seventeen...I *am* seventeen."

"You'll always be seventeen to me," he says.

"Why do you say that?"

"Because I'm always going to think of you exactly as you are right now," says Jimmy. He kisses my eyelids. "I think it works that way. Won't you feel that way about me when we're... I don't know?"

"Sixty-four?"

"Yeah," he says. "Sixty-four."

I run my hand down the side of his body. I kiss his chest, then look up at his face. "You're my one," I say. "My *THE* One."

"You're my one," he says.

I shake my head. "You don't have to say that just because I said it. I needed to say it...to hear it out loud. You're the one. Anybody else is just...in the way. Superfluous. Irrelevant. The not The One."

"I'm not just saying it," he says, surprising himself. "I mean it."

"I believe you," I say.

"Time will tell," he says as he lowers his lips to mine.

"What does time know?" I say.

I close my eyes and kiss him.

―

THE NEXT MORNING, THERE'S Jimmy sleeping next to me. Watching him sleep is its own kind of wonderful. I brush the hair from where it's fallen across his eye so I can see the swoop of his lashes. Ever so gently, I run the back of my index finger along the space between his eyebrows, the chisel of his jaw. He smiles.

"Good morning," he says without opening his eyes.

"Good morning."

"Let's stay in bed all day," he says.

"That sounds yummy."

He pulls me to him. My locket swings against his chin. He opens his eyes and catches the gold heart between his fingers. "Does it open?"

"It does."

He struggles to slip a fingernail into the groove to pry it open. I do it for him. He smiles at the picture inside. Joni, age two.

It's weird to show Jimmy Westwood a picture of Joni while we're naked in bed. Beyond weird. I haven't thought of her in hours, a day maybe. How is that possible? I'm a rotten mother, but—and here's the weirdest weird—I don't feel like a mother at all. Like when all those people injecting their bellies with weight loss meds talk about the massive brain real estate miraculously freed up when the food chatter disappears, suddenly there's all this space in my brain that's not exactly empty but not occupied either. Motherhood had a monopoly on a huge mental neighborhood and all those thoughts have gone on vacation.

"You haven't changed a bit," he says, smiling at the picture of Joni.

"No," I say. "Not really."

He studies the picture. "You look so happy."

Yes, that's a happy child.

"You've always been you," he says.

I snap the locket closed.

"No matter how I try to escape!" I laugh.

"You're still you."

"You're always you," he sings. He reaches for the guitar propped at the foot of the bed and starts to strum, exploring different melodies as he sings, "You're always you," morphing into "*You were always you…*" Then, "*You tried to escape, but you were always you…*"

It's starting to sound like a song. He sings it several times, adding phrases. "Promise you won't leave," he says.

My throat tightens. My chest flutters. I don't answer.

The door flies open. I whip the sheet up to my neck. Jimmy's unphased. It's that kind of house.

It's Royce. "Sounds good, man."

"Thanks," says Jimmy. "I think it might be something."

Royce picks up Jimmy's shirt from the floor and tosses it to him. "Get downstairs and lay this thing down on tape."

"We're busy here…" says Jimmy.

"I don't give a shit," says Royce. "Get your ass out of that bed and downstairs before you lose the song."

"Come on, man," says Jimmy.

"Don't act like that's never happened before. Losing the thread."

Jimmy looks at me. "It has happened before," he acknowledges sheepishly.

"Then get your ass downstairs," I say (without a hint of my crushing disappointment). "I'm fine."

Jimmy pulls the shirt over his head and steps into his jeans. "I'll be downstairs," he tells me.

"So I hear," I say.

He grabs his guitar, kisses me, and heads out.

Royce stays behind. "You know, Sunshine, you're always going to take second place."

"I know about Nina."

"I'm not talking about Nina."

"What?" I say, pulling the sheet up higher. "The groupies?"

Royce steps closer to the bed.

"Not Nina. Not the groupies. It's the stardom. It's a drug. And I see him getting hooked."

"That's a little melodramatic, don't you think?"

"I do not," he says. "We haven't gotten anywhere close to the melodramatic part yet."

"What's that supposed to mean?"

"It means I know Jimmy. And I know what he's willing to give up and what he's not willing to give up. And let's just say this. What he's not willing to give up is being a star because that, Sunshine, lets him hang onto the illusion that he can change the world."

"Maybe it's not an illusion."

He nods slowly and pushes the door almost shut. "I have a feeling you know better than that," he says, stepping closer to the bed.

"Hold the hashtag," I say. "There will be no *Me Too* moment here."

"Huh?"

"Just get out of here!" I don't mean to shout but I do.

Nina appears. "What's going on?"

"Nothing," says Royce. "Just having a little heart to heart."

She fixes me with her laser eyes.

"Jimmy's writing a song," I say. "He's downstairs."

Nina looks from Royce to me, me to Royce. She's filing away the visual: me in bed wrapped in a sheet, Royce standing inches away. It's a data point that might come in handy. Nina and I lock eyes. I've got lasers of my own.

"Now if you don't mind, I'd like to get dressed."

Alone in the room, I get out of bed and reach for my dress. I catch sight of myself in the old-fashioned full-length mirror standing in the corner—a giant rectangle suspended in a carved wooden frame. The kind that swings back and forth. Right now, it's tilted back at a fun-house angle. Part of my head is cut off and I'm all stretched out with crazy long limbs and a spindly neck. Like Alice after eating the cake.

I give the mirror a little tap to nudge it upright. There's my head, returned to my body, no longer akimbo. It's just plain old me. But somehow not. This is the me that Jimmy loves. The best possible me.

I slip the dress over my head. My locket rests against its sunset colors. I pluck the neckline away from my skin and let the necklace disappear under the fabric so that the string of thrift store love beads is all that shows.

I do a little pirouette in the mirror. Then I slip my camera over my neck and… Click. A Cheshire cat smile.

———

Downstairs, little has changed since the night before. The two girls on the sofa have shifted from toe-to-toe to toe-to-face. Sam is stretched out on the window seat smoking a joint. A half-naked girl sleeps nestled between him and the window.

"Where's Jennifer?" I whisper.

"At the house," he says.

"Isn't this the house?"

"The other house."

"What other house?"

Sam pushes himself up to sitting. "A bunch of chicks and their kids are living together over on Cole."

I remember she mentioned that. "What about you?' I wonder.

"I live here," he says, "most of the time."

"What about Tomorrow?"

"I'm not sure," he shrugs. "Might be here. Might crash somewhere else. Who knows."

"Your baby," I say. "Tomorrow."

He shrugs. "She's with Jen."

The strumming of a guitar pulls me into the dining room. Jimmy is perched on the edge of a low stool bent over his guitar. He strums the same chord a few times, humming a melody, then tries a different chord.

On the other side of the table, Royce sits on a high-backed velvet chair hovering over a behemoth of a tape recorder. (Must be what they call reel-to-reel because, duh, one reel feeds tape to the other reel). He presses a button on the machine and nods to Jimmy. Jimmy notices me in the doorway and smiles.

Royce follows Jimmy's eyes to me. He smiles, too, as if he means it. He's diabolically good at that, the creepy veneer of sincerity. "We'd love to play, Sunshine, but I'm afraid duty calls."

"I'm not going to bother you," I say. "I just wanted to let you know I'm going for a walk."

"You'll be back?" Jimmy says, making sure.

"Of course." I kiss him goodbye, my love beads clanking against his guitar.

As I head out, Royce says, "Okay, Jimbo, let's get back to it. The future is waiting."

"As long as you're not waiting for the future," I say.

Jimmy smiles. "Never," he says. "Tomorrow never knows."

"That's a good line for a song!" I say.

"Beatles," he says.

"Of course," I laugh.

CHAPTER NINE

THE LEICA HANGS AROUND my neck as I wander through the Haight.

A girl *grand jetes* down the street, a beatific smile lighting her way. Click.

On the next block a guy approaches me. He wears a fleece jacket, grease-smudged and torn. "Looking to get lifted?"

"I prefer Uber... Wait, what?"

"I got some good green."

"No thank you," I say in passing. "Green is not my color."

I cover some ground and find myself in front of the thrift shop. The sign in the window has been changed. It now reads, "Reduce, Reuse, Recycle." A flicker of pride—that was my mantra. But I'm not so great at living it. Pretty good about the recycling, but I could do better with the reducing and reusing. I make a silent pledge to try harder. I snap a picture of the sign. Click.

Bodhi waves me in through the window. He finishes scrawling on a piece of cardboard, then tapes it to a box: "Old Newspapers."

"Cool," I say. "And I like your new sign."

He looks up. "I kinda ripped you off."

"No problemo," I say. "How's school?"

"Boring. Tax law, contract law, finance..." He mimes a yawn, patting his gaping mouth. "I might drop out."

"How about environmental law?"

"What's that?"

"You know," I say, pointing at the newspaper box. "All the things you're interested in. Saving the planet."

"I don't think that's a law thing," he says.

It can't be that far off. "Is there something called Earth Day?" I ask.

"Isn't earth day every day?" he says.

"I mean, you know, Earth Day." I hit the words with emphasis. "Like it's not a holiday exactly, but one of those…I don't know…public awareness days."

"Never heard of it."

"I bet there will be," I say. "And when that happens, people will start talking more about the environment. And then…voila…they'll have to have environmental law… I'm guessing."

"Groovy," he says. "I could dig that."

"You could," I say. "And you should."

"What about you?" he asks. "You're a…junior?"

Nope. "Senior," I say. I pick up a candle carved like the sun.

"So you're into…" He nods toward the Leica around my neck, "…taking pictures?"

"Yeah…" I take a whiff of the candle. Somebody went a little nuts with the lavender.

"What do you like to shoot?" he asks.

"Good question," I say. What I like to shoot…what I do shoot…too complicated. I change the subject. "All that newspaper you're going to collect? You can use it as wrapping paper. Very hip." I head out.

He flashes me a peace sign and I wave goodbye.

The boy who usually works the counter at the Pall Mall isn't there today. I order my cup of coffee to go and wait.

"The fuzz are doing a sweep to pick up runaways," says a guy inhaling a stack of pancakes at the counter.

The guy on the next stool nods. "They think any dude without a draft card is an evader."

A pair of wire-rimmed glasses sits on the counter near the cash register. I pick them up. The lenses are pink.

"Somebody left 'em here," says the waitress heading over with my coffee. "You want 'em? They're yours."

I slip them on.

The counter gal hands me my coffee in a Styrofoam cup. I don't particularly want to get my caffeine fix from a carcinogenic container, but I could use a jolt, so I take a sip. I make a mental note to tell my buddy Bodhi that after newspaper recycling, he should get these cups banned. It's both good to know he's on the case and way depressing to realize how much more epic that case has grown since these days. When I come from, we're staring down the barrel of hopelessness. But hope springs eternal, even false hope. It makes no sense given our respective time frames, but Bodhi makes me feel hopeful.

Counter Gal offers me cream in the little ribbed-glass pitcher I remember. I pour some in and take a sip. Delicious. Everything you'd want from coffee without all the extra-shot, light-foam, flat-white frou-frou. Who needs the frou-frou? The frou-frou gets in the way.

1967 is not about frou-frou.

It's about tumult. Tumult is sort of its claim to fame. I had a history professor who called times like this GCTPs—Great Convulsive Transition Periods. The Fall of the Roman Empire, The Industrial Age, The Sixties. I understand. I get it. But walking down Haight in my flowy dress looking through crystal spectacles…I mean, literal rose-colored glasses…with my morning coffee in my hand and music pouring from every storefront, every apartment window, every passing car, I find myself smiling, buoyed by the spirit, the energy, the possibility.

How not me. Maybe GCTPs apply to individual people, too.

I look up to discover I'm standing at the corner of Haight and Cole. Sam said Jennifer lives on Cole. Maybe I can find her house. Like the Scarecrow in *The Wizard of Oz*, I randomly pick a direction and head up Cole, a sunny street lined with two- and three-story houses sporting bay windows. I spot one up ahead—faded Wedgewood blue with white trim. The front steps are littered with toys. Might as well give it a try. (Not like me to ring the doorbell of a strange house and ask if Jennifer can come out and play, but when in the Haight...)

A bevy of pretty young things skip toward the house next door to the blue one and scamper up the steps. A guy sits on the top step—small with shoulder-length brown hair and crazy wide eyes. Even from the sidewalk I can see the whites of his eyes all the way around. He stands and throws open his arms. The girls rush to claim a spot under them. Except one. She hangs back. He smiles at her. "Join the family."

I think better of asking if Jennifer lives next door. There's a strange vibe swirling around their whole scene. Besides, I'm pretty sure I have the right place because the sound of babies crying—more than one baby for sure—pours out of the blue house. I knock. A young woman opens the door. The baby on her hip has a crusty nose and wears nothing but a diaper. It hasn't been changed for a while—quite the stench.

"Is there a Jennifer here?" (I can tell the real me is back. I feel like an idiot.)

"Sure, come in." She calls over her shoulder, "Jennifer!"

Jennifer appears from the back of the house. "Mari!" She throws her arms around me. She's incapable of saying hello without the kind of hug that's usually reserved for a long-lost reunion. "Groovy specs! What are you doing here?"

"Sam said you were staying somewhere on Cole and I just got lucky."

She ushers me in. A flip-over chalkboard on a stand takes up one corner of the living room. Looks like potential danger to me. Beat-up wooden blocks lie scattered everywhere. A tree drawn in purple crayon covers one wall. A large rectangular table is covered with the remnants of various meals, cups of tea, and half-drunk baby bottles. The place kind of stinks—a rank mix of curry, yerba mate, and souring milk.

Jennifer leads me through the room into a sort of screened-in sunroom where a threadbare couch is piled with laundry. Two more full baskets sit to the side of the couch. I guess it's clean laundry, hard to tell. A few piles lie sorted on the table in front of the couch. Jennifer resumes her sorting. Mini T-shirts to her right, mini-socks to her left, diapers in the middle. All adult clothes stacked together on the floor in unfolded heaps. I plop myself on the other end of the couch, clean laundry between us, and start sorting. I'm slower than she is. I fold each item like I'm delivering it to a hotel guest.

A toddler wearing an undershirt and nothing else, no diaper, waddles in. Jennifer scoops him up for a quick kiss on his cheek. "This is Phoenix."

"Hi, Phoenix." Normally I would ask first but it seems entirely acceptable to reach out and squeeze his chubby thigh.

A girl about seven wanders in. "Phoenix!" she says, "I've been looking for you. Want a snack?"

Jennifer puts him down. Phoenix trails the little girl out of the room. "I made a fresh batch of granola," Jennifer calls after. She smiles at me. "Remember? You're the one who told me to call it granola…when my cookies crumbled." She crisscrosses her legs under her and continues to sort.

"Where's the baby?" I ask.

"Tomorrow? Taking a nap. I think."

"You're not sure?" I say it without thinking. Uncool, judgmental. Jennifer brings out the real me.

"Don't worry," says Jennifer. "Tara's doing nap time today."

I nod, though I'm equal parts relieved and worried. "So it's a whole commune kind of situation going on here?"

Jennifer shrugs. "It's just a bunch of us mothers raising our kids together."

"How does that work?"

"It doesn't have to work. It just is. Everyone does what everyone does and it all comes together."

"You don't miss…I don't know…bonding with Tomorrow on your own?"

"She knows I'm her mother."

"I didn't mean that."

"You did," says Jennifer, smiling, "and that's okay. I get it. We're trying something different."

Is life an experiment?

"I know what you're thinking," she says. "I was brought up the regulation way. I was raised by a mother who was in the house all the time and had homemade cookies and milk waiting when we got home from school." She catches her wavy hair into a leather cord and ties it at the back of her neck. "My mother was…"

"Happy?" I volunteer.

She shakes her head.

"Content?"

No.

"Fulfilled?"

Her eyes search for the right word. "Lonely," she says. "This works for both of us, Tomorrow and me. I like being around people. And Tomorrow…she won't have to worry she's—you know—everything to me. She doesn't belong to me. She's not here for me. She's here for her. It's her life. The more people who love her, the better her life will be."

"It takes a village," I say. "Like Hillary said."

"I don't know her. But…yeah."

I dump out another laundry basket and start sorting.

Two little girls chase each other into the room. "You be Princess Lolly," says one, "and I'll be Queen Frostine." They grab a couple of pillowcases and turn them into capes. Then they disappear.

They're smack in the sweet spot of the *Candy Land* age. Just like Joni. She'd fit right in. She could be Gramma Nutt.

A young woman walks in holding Tomorrow. Jennifer gathers the baby, nuzzles her, then offers her to me. "Wanna hold her?"

I take the baby in my arms and breathe deep the smell of her hair, her skin, her babyness. "She's so beautiful," I say.

"I know," says Jennifer.

"Enjoy this time. It's like you wake up one morning and someone's pressed fast-forward on this little girl."

She stares at me blankly.

"You know. Time speeds up. Birthdays blur by. She's only going to be this little for…" I snap my fingers.

"Would you like to live here with us?"

"Oh! I don't know…I mean, this is perfect for you. But I'm not sure…You know me…well, you sort of know me…actually, I think you know me pretty well…certainly enough to get that I'm not really a group person. Not much of a joiner."

"You'd be really good with us."

I try to picture myself living in this house with a bunch of women and their kids, newcomers drifting in and out, many abandoning the dream after a month or two and returning to Boise; Topeka; Gary, Indiana.

"You can come and visit anytime," says Jennifer.

"I wonder if I can."

"Of course you can. There's always room."

Jennifer watches me coochy-coo the happy baby. "She loves you."

"I love *her*," I say. I burrow my face into her neck. My chest constricts and my cheeks flush in a rush of something primordial. Suddenly, I miss Joni with a ferocity that feels like madness. My baby, my baby, my baby.

Tomorrow whimpers. Jennifer takes her from me. She lifts her peasant blouse and settles the baby into the crook of her arm. Tomorrow opens her mouth like a little bird and begins to nurse.

A flower child—twenty-ish and waif-like—wearing combat boots and a minidress appears from upstairs. She carries an infant in her arms and holds the baby so Jennifer can see.

"Does chickenpox look like this?" says Boots.

The baby's cheeks are bright red.

"Was she in the sun?" asks Jennifer.

I peer out through the porch screens. San Francisco overcast blankets the yard.

"Does she have a fever?" I feel the baby's forehead, then her flaming cheeks. She's hot. Like hundred-and-two hot. At least.

I snap into action. "Get the Tylenol. And maybe call 9-1-1."

"They have a phone next door."

"You don't have a phone?"

"Who are we supposed to call?" says Boots.

"9-1-1."

Blank stares.

"Just to be safe," I clarify.

Continuing stares.

"No 9-1-1?" I ask. How is that possible? What are you supposed to do? "Okay…okay…" I'm thinking. "Let's take her temperature."

"Do we have a thermometer?" says Jennifer.

"I'm not sure," says Boots. "She was a little warm like this yesterday. Slept a bunch. I thought she was getting a cold. But all of a sudden…"

"It looks like she got slapped across the face," I realize.

"I didn't hit her," says Boots, about to cry.

"Of course not," says Jennifer. She unlatches Tomorrow to lean in for a closer look at the red-faced baby.

"Slapped cheek rash," I clarify.

They stare at me.

"There's a childhood illness that has a rash like that. Listlessness, fever, rash. Fifth disease. My d…my little sister had it. Where's the Tylenol?"

"We've got baby aspirin," Jennifer volunteers.

"No!" I shriek. "Never give aspirin to kids."

They're so confused.

"Just take my word for it," I snap. "And let's cool her off." I take the baby from her mother and start to unwrap the swaddling. I can feel the heat rise off her.

"I'll put some elderflower in her bottle," says Boots.

I shake my head without looking up from the baby.

"Is this dangerous?" Boots is crying now.

"Any high fever can be dangerous."

Jennifer looks to me. I'm suddenly the authority. "Just call the pediatrician?" I offer.

"The clinic's got one," says Jennifer. "Sometimes."

"Let's give her a bath," I say.

Boots heads to the kitchen. Jennifer scoops up Tomorrow and we follow.

Boots runs the tap into the old farmhouse sink.

"Not hot, not cold," I say. Who cares if I'm a know-it-all.

The baby relaxes as she's settled in the water.

We all do.

I take Boots' hands and replace mine with hers against the baby's back.

—

OVER THE NEXT FEW hours at least a dozen people wander in and out of the house, some toting little kids, others borderline kids themselves.

I sample Jennifer's granola. I didn't realize I was so hungry. I eat fistful after fistful as she concocts a new batch, adding pumpkin seeds and dried apricots.

"You know," I say, "you may not have a lot in common with your mother, but you sure got the baking gene." I urge her to sell her granola, but she says something about how selling means selling out, so I let it go. (I don't have to push. After all, I have the advantage of knowing Miss Jennifer's Granola will find its way to specialty markets of the future.)

I stay long enough to make sure the slapped-cheek baby is better. Her cheeks look a little less bright and she laughs when her mommy plays peek-a-boo.

I grab a piece of paper and jot down: *Tylenol.* "That's how you spell it," I say. "You want the kind for kids." It's got to be available, right? Or maybe not. "Just remember that…whenever you see it at the store…"

Then Jennifer walks me out, cradling Tomorrow. She wraps a sweater around my shoulders. "It's Sam's. Give I back to him. If you see him."

One of the little Candy Land girls dashes out. "You forgot these!" She holds out the rose-tinted glasses.

"That's okay," I say. "You keep them. Queen Frostine should have them!" She slips the glasses on and flits off.

Outside, the same guy and his harem lounge on the front stoop of the house next door. Like most of the guys in the city, he's playing guitar.

"Hi, Charlie!" waves Jennifer.

"He looks familiar," I say.

"He's a songwriter," she says.

I nod. Isn't everyone?

"He's friends with the Beach Boys or something."

As I head down the street, I hear him holding court with the girls. "You know, a long time ago being crazy meant something. Nowadays everybody's crazy. Might as well be crazy in LA."

"LA?" wonders one of the girls.

"Why not?" he says. "You'll all come with me, right?"

"We'll follow you anywhere, Charlie," coos the girl rubbing his shoulders.

CHAPTER TEN

It's well into the afternoon, but the sun is just now burning through the fog. It beats down through a sky dotted with puffy clouds. I head for the Victorian. I sure am getting my steps in. The angle of the sun gives me a vice-at-the-temples headache. Or maybe it's that post-adrenaline migraine you get in the wake of being stressed. Heavy duty hyperdrive—that's where the whole sick baby thing sent me. So much those moms didn't have on hand. Baby monitor; white noise machine; the *What to Expect* parenting books. Mostly smarts. It's a wonder these commune situation babies survived. Not that I judge. But peace-and-love only gets you so far when your kid has a fever.

As I round the corner onto Ashbury, a girl whips off her top, an armload of bangles clanking as she pulls the blouse over her head. At least half the people I pass are barefoot. A couple of hippies make out in a doorway. Hot town, summer in the city.

But it's not summer anymore.

A wood-paneled station wagon with Ohio plates cruises by. Spraypainted across the back: GOD IS LOVE—SPEED KILLS.

Across the street, a homeless guy squats on a bedroll, hand outstretched. "Want me to read your I Ching?"

"No thanks," I say.

"C'mon, throw the Ching," he tries again. "It'll help you with the future."

"I like the future to be a surprise... And the past too." I take a few steps, then turn back to him. "Actually, I could use a reading of my future past... I mean my past future...whatever...go for it."

"For real?" Seems like he doesn't get a lot of takers.

"Sure."

He lays out his materials on the ground in front of him. Three coins; a big red book—*The Book of Changes*; a little notebook and a pencil. He gathers up the coins—not Chinese or anything exotic, just ordinary quarters—and drops them in my palm. I hesitate to make contact with his grubbiness, but oh well.

"Think about your question," he instructs me.

I didn't realize this was audience participation. "Do I have to say it out loud?"

"Up to you."

All my go-to questions belong to another time. But here I am. *Am I meant to be here?* That's my question. "Go ahead," I tell him.

"Okay. Throw them six times."

I throw them on the ground.

"Pick them up," he says, "and throw them again. Six times."

I do. That was one…now two, three, four, five, six times. With each toss, he mutters something about "a two, a two, and a three" or "a three, a three, and a two." There's other mumbo-jumbo about static yin and old yang as he scratches lines on a page in the notebook from the bottom up. Then he flips through the pages of the big handbook to find the match to the pattern of lines. The patterns are all pretty similar. He could pick the wrong one and I wouldn't notice. But he's a professional.

I'm Number 30. Woo-hoo!…I guess.

He turns to the interpretation of Number 30 and reads slowly. "The hexagram appearing in your casting means that you should shine a light on your thoughts and your intentions. Bring things into the open and let people see that you're about to do what you're doing."

He looks up at me. "Good one," he intones.

I'm not sure I get that last part about letting people see that you're about to do what you're doing. That's got some weird time thing going on. Then again, so do I.

"I pay whatever I want?" I ask, assuming he uses the coin of the realm.

"As long as it's a buck," he says.

That's seems like a lot to pay for voodoo given I could eat a burger for twenty-five cents, but I fish a dollar out of my pocket and drop it in the waiting hat. "Thanks," I say.

He shoves the bill in his pocket. I snap his picture, the empty hat in front of him. Click.

I head down Fulton.

As I near Haight, I spot Nina coming out of a restaurant on the corner. It's called Magnolia Thunderpussy. She's with an elegant older couple—not old-old, but definitely grown-ups. She sees me, too. And the older woman sees her see me. One of those moments where there's no escaping the smile-and-wave. I meet them at the corner.

"These are my parents," says Nina.

I'd assumed Nina was hatched fully cooked, hard-boiled. I never thought of her having parents. Especially these. A father in gray slacks and a pullover sweater; a mother in a skirt, twin set, and pearls.

Her mother stares at her, prompting.

"This is Mari," Nina acquiesces.

We go a round of "Nice to meet you."

Mrs. Nina's Mom smiles at me. "Do you two know each other from Miss Burke's?"

"Miss Burke's?" I laugh. Me? Everyone's heard of The Katherine Delmar Burke School. Expensive and posh. Very upper crust. Who's the girl with the fancy education now?

"No," snaps Nina.

I feel compelled to fill the silence. "We have mutual friends. The guys in Nina's band."

"Oh yes," says Mr. Nina's Dad. "Nina's little band."

Nina winces almost imperceptibly. She raises her hand to hail a cab.

"They're fantastic!" I say. "They have a hit record, you know." Look at me—hyping Nina. Only to her parents.

"Nina used to model in the tearoom at I. Magnin," says Mrs. Nina's Mom, as though that were a higher calling than music. I've never heard of I. Magnin but I get the picture. And of course she did. Nina's model-beautiful.

A taxi pulls to the curb. Nina can't open the back door fast enough.

"Thanks for lunch," she says, ushering her parents toward the open door. They both give her cheek a peck before sliding in. Then the cab pulls away.

We stare at each other, Nina and I.

"Your parents are still together?" I say.

"So they tell me. Marriage… It's a beat-up old institution."

"Or it's an old institution that beats you up," I say.

We stare at each other some more. The truth is the two of us have only one thing in common and we're not going anywhere near Jimmy…conversationally.

Nina turns on her heels.

I call to her back. "What do you think this means: *Let people see that you're about to do what you're doing?*"

She stops in her tracks, turns around. Her eyes narrow. "It means: give a person fair warning." Then she struts off.

MUSIC SPILLS OUT OF every house in the neighborhood. Jimmy's Victorian included. Something Latin—salsa, probably—from P.J.'s window; cool jazz from Boo-Boo's; acoustic folk from Sam's—a simple melody, if haunting, with lyrics that wear their heart on their sleeve. *"It's always the old to lead us to the wars / Always the young to fall / Now look at all we've won with the saber and the gun / Tell me, is it worth it all?"* Could be Bob Dylan, but no, I don't think so.

It's like the inner workings of a bunch of music boxes got jumbled together in one big, perpetually wound music box. That's the Neon Dream house…and so many others.

When I enter, Royce's voice cuts through all the music loud and clear. "I don't want ten half songs. Ten half songs are useless to me. I'll take one finished song to start with. Right now. I need one whole song."

Royce pounds away at Jimmy. They are exactly where I left them, the tape recorder sitting idle between them on the dining room table. Jimmy lights up when he sees me. There's no better feeling. He crosses to the foyer and kisses me, then leads me into the dining room by the hand.

"Hello, Sunshine," Royce growls.

I roll my eyes. It's more efficient than launching a verbal response.

"We're talking business," he says to Jimmy.

"She stays," says Jimmy.

Again, no better feeling.

I set my camera on the table, then remove Sam's sweater and hang it on the back of a chair.

Now it's Royce who rolls his eyes.

"You know you can do this, Jimmy," I say, "I have complete faith in you. But you have to do it in your own way, in your own time." I turn to Royce: "It's a process. You can't turn on inspiration like a faucet." I have no firsthand knowledge of this, of course.

I step closer to Jimmy. "The songs have to come to you…or something like that. They're out there."

"He's been processing all day," says Royce snidely.

Go ahead, mock my day.

"He's afraid we're going to be a one hit wonder," says Jimmy.

"Did the person who came up with the phrase 'one hit wonder' ever come up with anything else?" I say, hoping a little levity will shift the mood (a very little levity).

Jimmy offers a wan smile.

Royce stands. "This isn't fun and games anymore. He's a professional now. Be grateful there's a demand for more Neon Dream." He takes a step toward Jimmy. "Your job is the supply. Supply and demand, baby. That's the game." Royce turns to me like Jimmy isn't in the room. "He's got obligations."

That one gets to Jimmy. "Hey, man, this was never supposed to be about obligations."

"Welcome to the real world," says Royce. "You signed a contract with a record company. And it's got a delivery date on it right there along with your John Hancock. Time to grow up."

Jimmy shakes his head. Growing up—that's a low blow.

"Come on, Jimmy." Royce presses RECORD on the tape recorder. "There's no time like the present."

"That's not necessarily true," I say. "And may I add, artists don't ever really grow up. Playing is their work. Part of the process…"

"There you go again. Don't give me this process shit."

"Part of the artistic process," I repeat, drawing out the word just to rankle him, "is staying in touch with your inner child." (A gag-able phrase, but I'm vamping for time. And having sacrificed my own inner child to take pictures of overpriced houses, I feel semi-qualified to climb onto this particular high horse.)

"Spare me," says Royce.

Jimmy puts his head in his hands, defeated. "He's right. I got nothing. I'm empty."

I kneel down and take his face in my hands. "Okay…this isn't easy. But nothing worthwhile ever is. This is how you felt before you wrote 'Moonlight.'"

Honestly, I don't know how to play this. Knowing how things unfold should be an advantage, like with Jennifer and her granola success. But I can't say what the future holds. Not for sure. I could take a stab, but it might be wrong since the future I know—the future where he performed at that One Hit Wonder concert in

2011—may not include the effects of this trip that I'm on right now. It's entirely possible that on this visit, I'm supposed to change things.

Here's an obvious: I did plenty of research after my first trip to 1967. I know about the grandfather paradox. (You travel back in time, prevent your grandfather from meeting your grandmother, thereby preventing your own birth. Then how could you travel back in time?) I know about coexistent multiple timelines. (You travel back in time, create new timelines, but don't alter your own.) I even know about the self-consistency principles. (You travel back in time, but your actions are constrained by the events that led you to your time travel in the first place.) And of course there's *Back to the Future*. They all have their points. And they all make your head explode. Bottom line: if physicists, philosophers, and Marty McFly can't figure this out, how can I?

So…if I sift together the various theories, add a splash of optimism, and bake, maybe I can change Jimmy's destiny? If I inspired him to write one great song last time, maybe I can inspire him to write an album's worth of great songs this time. Or at least enough songs for an album.

"You told me music can change the world," I tell him with conviction. "Maybe if you write a song about all the things that could be better…like a letter to the world…"

Royce has heard enough from me. "Jimmy, you're going to listen to this kid?" He turns to me. "Where'd you run away from anyway?"

I ignore him. He keeps going.

"Jimmy," he continues, "the label is getting antsy. Fans have short attention spans. We don't have time for you to wait for inspiration. Go upstairs, have your fifteen minutes with her, and come back down with your head screwed on, man."

I face Royce. "The world is full of people like you. Everything has to be fast. Boom, boom, boom. Who cares about quality as long as the content gets out there. Feed that content monster twenty-four-seven!" My voice shoots up a few octaves. "Keep it coming! Swipe left, swipe right! That's not going to get his band to Woodstock. And let's face it, if they can get to Woodstock, they'll be etched in history."

"Where the fuck is Woodstock?"

"That's not the point."

People wander in to see what the crazy girl is ranting about. P.J. and Boo-Boo and a couple of random girls stand in the doorway. Having an audience doesn't stop me. I bore into Royce.

"You're all about the transaction, aren't you? Every little bit of life has to be transactional. Don't do anything for the joy of it, pure and simple. Oh no, that's not the point. Quid pro quo. That's the point." I take a step closer to Royce like he did to me upstairs. "You, my friend, are going to go far. There's a world out there waiting for people like you. Be patient. The eighties are coming. I think it's the eighties...whenever...but I guarantee you there's a decade out there with your name on it. And then you'll be home free. King of the castle."

I take another step toward Royce. I'm standing inches away. Now who's moving in for the kill, mister? He rubs his hands on his leather pants.

"I know your type. You're all over the socials, drooling for likes to make you feel like you've got this fabulous sparkly life. But guess what? It's all a sham. You've got nothing to sell. Except Jimmy... someone who wants to change the world...one heart at a time. You don't care about changing the world. Or maybe changing it one avatar at a time, in whatever way greases your already greasy pockets. You've got no talent. Zero. So you've latched onto real talent..." I place a hand on Jimmy's shoulder. "And all you care about is running him through the sausage machine and turning him into product."

P.J. turns to Boo-Boo. "Dig her."

"I remember," says Boo-Boo.

"Mind-benders," P.J. explains to one girl. "They're kind of her thing."

Jimmy stands to sling an arm around my shoulder. I'm almost done. "So…that's the polar route answer to your question. I didn't run away *from* anywhere. I ran *to* here. I was looking for Jimmy. I ran *to* Jimmy." There, I said it.

Jimmy tightens his arm around me, draws me closer to his side.

I take a deep breath, still glaring at Royce. "Any further questions?"

Nina appears with the smitten A&R guy at her side. "What the fuck is going on in here?" she snarls.

Boo-Boo laughs.

Royce spins the tape from one reel to the other, lifts the full reel off the spindle, and shoves it in the pocket of his fringed jacket—the whole exercise a charade since he just got through complaining about how nothing of use got recorded.

"Nothing's going on," Royce tells Nina. "Just straightening out some business."

I nod and smile. Butter wouldn't melt.

Royce nods at one of the girls, strides out of the dining room with her in tow, through the foyer, and out the front door. He slams it so hard the chandelier crystals clink against each other overhead.

"What the fuck?" says Nina, shaking her head. She turns on her heels and heads to the parlor. A&R follows like a puppy.

"That was something," says Jimmy.

"Something good? Or something bad?" I wonder.

"Something to behold," he says.

"I couldn't stop myself. He doesn't understand artists. He doesn't understand you. But it's really none of my business."

"It is your business," says Jimmy. "I'm your business." He kisses my forehead. "You're my hero. My perfect hero."

"I'm nobody's hero, believe me," I say. "And I'm so not perfect. I'm not perfect with a vengeance."

"Perfect's no fun anyway."

"No?"

He shakes his head no.

"I'm starving," he says. He takes my hand and leads me into the kitchen where several girls are preparing dinner. No guys. The guys are just standing around. Just saying. Jimmy commandeers them to gather chairs and carry them out to the backyard.

Jade Eyes smiles at me patronizingly like I'm a toddler slumped in a heap after a tantrum. My tirade must have carried into the kitchen, at least the high notes. I pitch in, grabbing silverware out of a drawer and filling random pitchers with water straight from the tap, as in plain old tap water. Jade Eyes dips a ladle into a pungent chickpea stew simmering on the antique stove, a heavy white enamel thing that dominates the kitchen. She pours it into a tureen, its rim ringed with pink rosebuds—someone's grandmother's Sunday china.

A freckled girl slides a loaf of bread out of the oven. It smells like hearth and home, at least the way hearth and home are supposed to smell. It makes my stomach rumble. Nothing works up an appetite like making a scene.

Another girl, a tiny pixie with a dark bob and cat-eye glasses, tears lettuce into a giant wooden bowl. "I'm late," she says to Jade Eyes. "Do you think I should follow Alex to Canada?"

"Ask Alex," Jade Eyes shrugs.

I consider telling the girl about the house on Cole where Jennifer and Tomorrow live with all those other mothers and kids, but "ask him" is a good start. She's probably not pregnant anyway.

I carry the water pitchers out back to where Jimmy and the guys have arranged the chairs around the long table, already stocked with bottles of wine and six-packs of beer.

Freckled Girl and Pixie emerge with the bread and salad. Jade Eyes appears in the doorway calling us in. We migrate back into the kitchen to serve ourselves from the big tureen before settling outside at the table.

Smoke signals must have gone up. The entire block seems to know that Sunday dinner is here for the taking. People arrive through the back door like clowns out of a VW bug. They're happy to sit on the ground.

Nina and A&R huddle at the opposite end of the table from Jimmy and me. Royce may call himself the band's manager, but Nina is the brains...and the cunning. She sidles closer to A&R so that their shoulders are touching. She whispers in his ear as he laughs and nods. I was utterly intimidated by her when I was here before, awestruck by her confidence. And guess what? Regardless of how old I actually am, everything about Nina still cows me. She emanates something that all the life experience in the world could never impart. To quote Lady Gaga, she was born that way.

I catch Boo-Boo raising an eyebrow at P.J., thrilled to see Nina working her magic on A&R. That can only be good for the band. I wonder if her truer motive is to make Jimmy just the tiniest bit jealous...or the not so tiniest bit.

Dinner stretches into the night. Candles are lit along the center of the table. Stragglers continue to float in, helping themselves to food. Newcomers arrive with armloads of vegetables—carrots and chard and onions shooting with sprouts. These they toss into the pot, like the storied stone soup. Pretty soon there's not a chickpea left in the incredible morphing veggie stew.

When I go back inside to refill the pitchers, I find P.J. rummaging in the flour canister. He jerks out his hand when he sees me. He's clutching a fistful of bills.

"What's up?" I say.

"Nothing."

"You sure?"

"We keep a little cash around..." he stammers. "You know, for emergencies..."

"What's the emergency?"

"Gotta lace up my axe." His hair is slick with sweat. He might be shaking.

"You okay?" I ask.

"I'm fine," he assures me. "Blood sugar thing. Gotta eat."

"P.J.…?" I prod.

He's out the back door in a flash but sticks his head back in. "Do me a favor. Don't tell the guys… They're always bitching at me to ease up or I'll snap my strings." Then he bounces back into the yard.

I hold the pitcher under the tap. I didn't actually promise P.J. I wouldn't say anything. I need to tell Jimmy. But when I go back outside, I find my seat occupied. A new girl with long black braids and a flower tucked behind her ear has cozied up to him. She wears a tank top, bra-free—very. He doesn't seem to mind. Especially when she laughs and touches his arm, letting it rest there too long. I scan the yard for an empty chair—preferably next to another guy, preferably cute, preferably cute enough to make Jimmy sweat. No chairs.

I stride over and set the pitcher in front of Braids.

"I'm sitting here," I declare.

She looks to Jimmy for confirmation. "Yeah," he says to her, "Mari's sitting here." She smiles at me as she stands, then drifts around the table until she lands on Sam's lap. He definitely doesn't mind. She rubs her bare arms with her hands; he takes off his sweater—the one Jennifer had given me—and wraps it around her.

Jimmy rests his arm across the back of my chair, leans over and kisses me on the temple. I glance at Braids across the table to see if she noticed. I think she did. Not proud of how happy that makes me.

Someone cranks up the radio. A guy wearing John Lennon glasses arrives carrying a massive sheet cake. "Happy Birthday Bob" is written across the top in blue script.

"I swung by to pick up some Digger bread, dig? 'Cause you know, I don't have any bread and they give you bread for free, and they were giving this thing away 'cause whoever ordered it never showed."

"Wow!" says one of the girls.

"We're having a birthday party!" says another.

"Who wants to be Bob?" says another.

I turn to Boo-Boo. "Your name is Bob!"

All eyes on me, especially Boo-Boo's. "How do you know?" he says.

"Oh! You told me."

"I did?" Boo-Boo scrunches his face, trying to remember.

"Obviously," I say. "How else would I know?" I deflect by launching into an overly enthusiastic version of *Happy Birthday*. Everyone joins in with a big emphasis on "Happy Birthday dear *Bob*!" Boo-Boo picks up a knife and is poised to cut when…

"Wait!" says Braids from Sam's lap. "We need a candle. We've got to do the wish thing."

Jade Eyes lifts one of the heftier candles from the middle of the table. It's at least four inches in diameter. She plops it in the center of the cake. It sinks in, frosting splurging.

"That's what I'm talkin' 'bout!" says P.J.

Freckled Girl claps her hands in an excited flurry. "We all have to make a wish!"

Everyone leans in toward the flame flickering with a golden glow in the darkness. Several close their eyes as they dig deep for their heart's desire. So do I. I close them so tight.

Jimmy counts down, "One…two…three!"

Together, we blow out the candle.

Pixie Girl claps. "The universe has to hear that kind of energy!"

Boo-Boo cuts the cake into great slabs. Everyone eats it with their hands, licking frosting from their fingers and from other people's fingers too. Jimmy licks mine and something quivers in me.

Someone turns up the radio. A solid, heavy beat drives this song. "*I've been waiting so long / To be where I'm going / In the sunshine of your love.*" A few people start to dance—swaying, spiraling, spinning.

The next song charges out of the radio. "*Manic depression is searching my soul / I know what I want but I just don't know / How to go about gettin' it.*" By the third verse, everyone is up and dancing. One girl undulates, another twirls. A guy bobs his head, eyes closed, at one with Hendrix. The backyard is transformed into a mini version of one of those Be-In's in the park—everyone dancing, everyone grooving. Embarrassingly, there's no other word.

Jimi sings the last "*Music sweet music sweet music…*" and the next song starts.

"*Tonight…*" And I freeze.

"*I know that being with you was meant to be / Tonight…I look into your eyes, my soul I see…*" It's "Tamara Moonlight." It's Neon Dream. It's Jimmy and Nina, their voices dissolving together into a single voice—part smoke, part honey. There's Jimmy with the melody, gentle and soothing, bringing the warmth. There's Nina layering the harmony, husky and textured, bringing the edge.

The yard erupts. We all whoop and cheer through the first verse. Jimmy looks down at the ground, shaking his head in disbelief and soaking up the sound of his song, of *him*, on the radio. Boo-Boo can't help but tap out the beat with his feet, his arms twitching for a cymbal. Nina closes her eyes and cocks her head, listening deeply. By the second verse, people dance slowly now, swaying and rocking to the song's gentler groove.

Jimmy looks up, offers me his hand. I take it, stand, and we dance. Almost formally, like in proper boy-girl dance position. I've heard this song my entire life. In the most mind-exploding of all the temporal paradoxes, this song was written for me *and* I was named for this song. But tonight, right now, it's my song more than ever. Because tonight, right now, it's our song.

"Wishes do come true," whispers Jimmy, embarrassing himself. "Dumb, huh?"

I shake my head no and rest it against his chest. His heart beats in time to the song. "We're making up for lost time," I say.

"It's been crazy," he says, "but it hasn't been all that long."

"No," I say. "I guess not. Not really."

Our bodies press against each other, our movements synchronize. *Stella by starlight belongs to yesterday / Tamara by moonlight is here to stay.*"

The yard erupts with cheers and applause.

The deejay takes a beat before speaking. The song demands that.

Jimmy leads me to the well-worn wicker swing—a two-seater—hanging from a branch of the giant tree in the corner of the yard, a Sycamore I think. The swing is missing one of its cushions, so we sit together on the single cushion as close we can get, his arm around me, my head resting on his shoulder.

"What do I have to do to make sure you stay?" he says.

I wish I knew.

"Is it something parental?"

We're both facing forward so he doesn't see me smile. "You might say that."

"I do great with parents," he says.

Would he still be great with me if he knew I'm the parent?

Fog is settling over the yard, clinging to the higher branches of the tree as we swing gently back and forth beneath. Jimmy tightens his arm around my shoulder, pulling me closer to his body against the chill.

"You'd be surprised," he says. "I clean up pretty well."

"You shouldn't change for anyone."

Jimmy takes a beat. He knows who I'm talking about. "Royce is okay. He made us a good deal with the label. He's good at that kind of thing, the stuff I'm no good at. He's got a whole plan."

"I'm sure he made a great deal. But he only cares about the money. You were never in it for the money."

"I know. He's helping us. Really. He's doing what's best for the band."

"Royce does what's best for Royce."

Jimmy says nothing.

"You used to know that," I add.

Again, nothing.

"We don't need to talk about it anymore," I say, showing uncharacteristic restraint. "I just don't trust him. I haven't trusted him since the minute I met him." So much for restraint.

"At least he's going to stick around," says Jimmy.

A shiver shoots through me.

"He's in it for the long ride," says Jimmy. "Next week, next month."

I want to tell him that I am, too. But I don't. I can't.

From the radio, a song so surging, so throbbing, so whirling, I wonder if someone put something in the stew. *"If you were a bird and you lived very high / You'd lean on the wind when the breeze came by / You'd say to the wind as it took you away / That's where I wanted to go today…"* The yard pulses with dancing. A guy and a girl hook up right there on the lawn in the middle of the yard, oblivious to the gyrating around them.

A few more couples move inside as the song ends. A smooth, husky voice speaks from the radio. "This is Dusty Street. Fly low and avoid the radar."

Another deejay takes the mic. "Hi there, groove-meisters, this is Tom Hudson coming to you from KSAN radio in far out San Francisco. I've got some bittersweet news to share. It's with heavy hearts that we bid farewell to a local institution. You all know it. Frizzie's is closing its doors after tonight. So tonight I'm celebrating some of the folks Frizzie introduced us to. From folk troubadours to the psychedelic sounds that define our city, Frizzie's has been a sanctuary for our souls. So, my fellow music lovers, let's recall the memories made, the magic conjured, the music that will echo in our hearts. And, if you can, stop by Frizzie's over on Belvedere and wish that badass goofball happy travels."

"I can't believe it!"

"When did that happen?"

"Where are we gonna hang?"

Mass exodus. Everyone heads into the house and through to the street, leaving the remnants of the night behind. Empty wine bottles, dirty dishes, cigarette butts, roaches.

"Happy travels," says Jimmy. "That's a song."

"I told you," I say as we climb out of the swing and head inside. "Songs everywhere."

Inside, he goes straight for his guitar and plops onto the sofa.

"Don't you want to go?" I say. "To Frizzie's?"

"You go ahead," says Jimmy. "I think I've got something."

Why would I go without him? I plunk down into an easy chair as Boo-Boo blasts in. "Aren't you coming?"

"Mari, you should go," Jimmy tells me. "Maybe I'll come later. Wish Frizzie happy travels on this planet earth…happy travels, sweet horizons." He's spinning lyrics already. "You guys go." He digs in his pocket and hands Boo-Boo the key to the van.

I grab the Leica and head out with Boo-Boo. "Lucky me! I get to go with the birthday boy!" He laughs and we climb into the van.

"I'm onto you," he says.

Instant cotton mouth.

"Oh yeah," he says. "I'm hip to you."

My mind races, but I've got nothing.

"Did your mother teach you to do stuff like that?"

"My mother!"

"Or your dad…or whoever told you it was okay to snoop in people's wallets."

"I didn't…"

"C'mon. I haven't told anyone my real name since I started playing drums. The first time I stuck a Band-Aid on a blister, it was bye-bye Bob, hello Boo-Boo. When I signed the contract, I didn't even let the other guys watch."

I exhale. "Your driver's license…"

"Robert Alan Abernathy."

"Quite the moniker," I laugh. "I thought it was Jimmy's," I improvise. "His wallet, I mean. He needed a five. He thought there was one in his wallet…"

"Forget it," he says. "For real. Forget it."

"Forgotten."

The drive through the Haight feels different at night. Police sirens echo through the streets, shrieking to the beat of bongos thumping somewhere. The smell of weed and incense, patchouli and falafel, give off an acrid undertone like garbage and urine. I roll up—literally crank up—the window of the van.

Outside the Free Clinic, there's a line down the block. STDs, ODs, bad trips—plenty of reasons for staying open all night. I raise my camera to my eye. Click.

Flickering neon signs, some missing a letter or two, illuminate a series of battered metal trash cans lining the sidewalk. Charred planks of wood jut out from them at cockeyed angles, the remnants of the coffin from that funeral—Death of the Hippie. I raise my camera to my eye. Click.

I turn my lens to Boo-Boo's profile. Click.

"I don't think I ever asked how you got into the drums," I say.

"I wouldn't say I got into the drums. I was just always banging on something. Drove my grandma nuts. Pots and pans with a wooden spoon. Anything. That's all I ever wanted to do. No toys for me. I broke a whisk banging on a pot. Grandma got so mad. Then she bought me a toy drum. It's one of my first memories."

My mind ping-pongs back and forth between the guy driving the van and my mother's husband, this drummer in a rock band and the drummer for hire if and when he lands a gig as a studio musician.

"I thought the coolest thing would be to be known for a beat. My own personal beat named for me."

"That's a thing?"

"Like the Bo Diddley beat." He pounds on the steering wheel, using the dashboard to accent the downbeat.

Why haven't I had this conversation with Bob? It's humiliating to keep learning the same lesson over and over. The people in your life have interesting stories to tell: ask them.

By the time we get to Frizzie's, there's a crush of people at the door. I bet he's never had a night this good.

Inside, the place is call-the-fire-marshal packed. It's crazy dark. Black light posters glow from behind the bar. Patches of feeble candlelight don't make much of a dent in the darkness, and the string of fairy lights that once provided atmosphere is mostly burnt-out bulbs.

Partiers have been drinking and passing joints all night. The place is lit. Everyone here is sloshed AF.

The crew from the Victorian filters in, along with the rest of the neighborhood—everyone grooving to the group on stage. *"You thought you had me baffled / You thought I didn't know / But I know what you're putting on / Long before you go."* They've got kind of a jug band sound, but they're dressed like they work behind the bar at an Old West saloon. Flat straw hats, arm garters, vests. Victorian? Edwardian? Some era that's long before this one.

Boo-Boo and I thread our way through the crowd to the stage. When the band finishes their song, one of the guitarists takes the mic. He thanks Frizzie for all the good times. "If it hadn't been for Frizzie in the early days, there'd be no Charlatans!"

I look to Boo-Boo questioningly.

"That's them. The Charlatans. Gonna be huge."

I've never heard of them, but I enthuse, "Really? Good for them!"

"Oh yeah," says Boo-Boo. "The Charlatans are the real thing."

"Very punny," I say.

I might see a flash of recognition dart across his face—an unsettling mix of premonition and déjà vu—like he's heard someone say that before or knows he'll hear someone say it in the future. Then again, I might not. I tend to project.

Frizzie takes the stage and introduces the next act. A folk duo called Hedge and Donna. Never heard of them. She's black, he's white, they're both gorgeous. Donna has a medium afro and wears a colorful long dress. A dashiki…or a muumuu. I'm not sure of the difference. Hedge is tall and lean and has what in 2024 would be a two-hundred-dollar haircut but now must simply be the luck of great hair. He also has cheekbones for miles. Did I mention: gorgeous—both of them.

The place falls reverentially quiet. Hedge strums his acoustic guitar, and they begin to sing. *"Let the sun-rain fall and let the dewy clouds enfold you / And maybe you can sing to me the words I just told you."* Their voices are as breathtaking as they are; their harmonies folksy and bluesy, layered and seamless. The soundtrack to a dream. *"If all the things you feel ain't what they seem / Then don't mind me 'cause I ain't nothin' but a dream…"* Click.

By the time they finish the song, I'm crying. I don't know why. But there's something pure about their sound, something pure about the way they look at each other that makes me unable to stop. Boo-Boo throws a brotherly arm around me.

"I don't know where that came from," I say.

"You don't have to," he says. "It's always a good thing when tears find their way out."

I've heard him say that before…to Joni. Now I'm the one with the weird deja-vu/premonition mash-up.

On stage, Hedge and Donna thank Frizzie for keeping his door open over the years. They wrap him in a bear hug.

Frizzie steps to the mic. "What's big and purple and lives in the ocean?" he says.

"Moby Grape!" shouts the crowd.

Five guys with muttonchops and shaggy Beatles's haircuts set up. Frizzie mingles with the crowd. He winds his way to Boo-Boo and me.

Boo-Boo shakes his head. "I can't believe this is it."

"You know what they say," says Frizzie. "All good things must come to an end."

"Too soon, man," says Boo-Boo.

"What made you decide?" I ask.

Frizzie shrugs. "Landlord's jackin' up the rent. Couldn't bring myself to charge all the folks I let in for free over the years."

Thrift store Bodhi pats Frizzie on the back. "What are you going to do with yourself, Frizz?"

"No clue."

"Good place to start," says Boo-Boo.

"Sorry you guys couldn't do a set tonight," Frizzie says.

"Us?" Boo-Boo's baffled.

"Royce said no," says Frizzie. "Didn't want to distract Jimmy from jammin' out some songs."

"Sounds like big daddy," says Boo-Boo. "Bummer."

Frizzie gets swept into another circle of well-wishers.

A surfer type makes his way over to Boo-Boo. "Dude!" he says, smacking him on the back. "You still in the market for a Black Beauty?"

"For sure."

My eyes widen. I'm assuming that's some sort of mind-altering substance, but I didn't know Boo-Boo was into hard drugs.

"I'm goin' down to TJ to hang loose for a spell. Gettin' rid of a lot of shit," says Surfer Dude.

"Cool," says Boo-Boo.

"It's in the car."

"Let's do it," says Boo-Boo.

"This baby's got a cutting crack you won't believe," says Surfer Dude as Boo-Boo follows him out.

"I'm going to have to find a ride home," I say to Bodhi. "He can't drive if he's all…" I spin my fingers around my temples for lack of a more creative way to demonstrate tripping out.

Bodhi laughs. "I think Black Beauty's a drum."

"A drum?"

"Like Ringo's."

"Oh! Well…I'm an idiot," I say.

"You make idiot look adorable," he says. Whoa.

"So… Thrift store… Law school… You're in a band too?"

"No," he says. "I just hang around musicians. I wouldn't have time with school and everything."

"Not dropping out after all?"

"No, I'm not. I didn't want to be…like, working for the man," says Bodhi. "But then I thought… You know those horror flicks where it's like, holy shit, it's coming from inside the house? That's what I'm going to do. That's going to be me. I'm going to come from inside the house." He smiles, then adds, "An inside job. An inside-the-system job."

Silence. It might be a charged with some sort of…attraction.

"I'm happy to give you a ride home anyway," he says. "I mean, even if Boo-Boo's not on drugs."

"Thanks," I say. "Not necessary."

"But fun?" That smile again.

"Fun can totally be fun." Who says things like that? Apparently, me.

Bodhi flicks my hair behind my shoulder. This is turning into a moment. Why am I enjoying it so much? I cock my head to the side like I'm one of those girls.

Then he leans in and whispers something. The music's too loud for me to hear. But I get the gist. And it has nothing to do with recycling. Thank God no one can see my cheeks turn magenta in the darkness.

"I'm sorry," I say, in over my head. "I didn't mean…"

Now he's flustered. He takes a step back and shakes his head like he misread the signal I was sending. Was I sending a signal? Do I even know how to do that?

"Sorry," he says. "Can we just turn the clock back three minutes?"

"Sure. Three minutes should be easy."

He laughs.

"My bad," I say.

"You do come up with the best way of putting things," he chuckles. "I'm gonna use that one, too."

We're both relieved to shift our gaze to the stage where Moby Grape is breaking into full-blown psychedelia. A guy in the back of the club has rigged up a makeshift light show. It surges with the music: "*Hey, Grandma, you're so young / Your old man's just a boy…*"

I think about saying good night and Ubering back to the Victorian—strike that, no Uber—but the band launches into a free-wheeling instrumental jam that sweeps me along. Despite being a confirmed non-joiner, riding this musical wave with a roomful of people makes me feel part of something. The bass thumps in my chest as it thumps in everyone else's. The guitar tingles across my skin as it tingles across everyone else's. The drumbeat synchronizes all our heartbeats.

I stay for the Grape's entire set. After that, random musicians take the stage in random combinations. The evening gets sloppy with speeches and toasts and Frizzie's farewell. He swipes the back of his hand across his eyes. Click.

Boo-Boo can't stop talking about his new snare drum on the drive home. He's always wanted a Ludwig Black Beauty and he's psyched.

He drops me at the Victorian and goes to find parking. I expect everyone to be asleep. But there's Royce, stretched out on the sofa in the parlor, wide awake, with a couple of deadbeat guests passed out on the floor. "Hey, Sunshine, I'm happy to see you."

Yeah, right.

He sits up. "You and I got off on the wrong foot. I'd like to make things right."

I step into the parlor, but I don't sit. Quick escape is always a good option when you're in a room with Royce.

He continues. "I wish you'd give me a chance. I've changed since the summer." He shakes his head. "You got me pegged. When our boy won the Battle of the Bands, I finally had to admit I don't have the talent. What I'm good at is making introductions. And deals. I know that's not the same kind of talent as Jimmy's talent, but it earns me my cut."

So he's realized he's a businessman. Big whoop.

"I've grown up a lot," he adds.

"Haven't we all?"

"And we're all here for the band, right?"

"I'm listening."

"Jimmy's been working all night," he says. "He might be onto a pretty decent track. You were right."

"I was?"

"The whole rap about process and shit."

I nod.

"Friends?" he ventures.

It's dramatically unlike me to grant second chances, much less make friends, but he's right. We *are* all on the same team. Maybe it's the leftover bonhomie from the communal buzz at Frizzie's, but I can't help but smile. "Okay," I say, "friends."

Royce smiles. For once, it doesn't look like a smile with an agenda. "Jimmy's on a roll," he nods upstairs.

I head up, move quietly down the hall. A muffled sound from Jimmy's room. I open the door.

There he is. In bed with Jade Eyes. They sit bolt upright when they see me, just like in the movies, but she doesn't bother to cover herself. *Au contraire.* She simply smiles at me and offers a demure little wave.

Jimmy's out of bed in a flash. "This isn't what it looks like." Again, right out of a B-movie.

"No?" I say. I exhale against the doorjamb.

He yanks on his jeans. "This is just... It just comes with the territory."

"This is not my territory," I say. "I don't know how I could have possibly thought this could ever be my territory." Jimmy and I lock eyes. He can see it. I'm flattened, undone.

He did that.

"I don't need this," he says. "I'm out of here." He storms out as though he's the injured party, leaving me alone with Jade Eyes. She gets out of bed and starts assembling herself. She veils herself in gossamer—long gauzy skirt; voluminous, flowy top—so sheer you can trace the outline of her body underneath. She can't find the mate to a giant hoop earring.

"Listen..." she says. "What are you? Sixteen? Seventeen? You don't know how guys are. They're...they're guys."

"I know about guys," I say.

She smiles condescendingly. After all, she's all of twenty-one... maybe.

"Jimmy's different," I say.

"Jimmy's a guy. That's all."

"And I suppose love is free?" I say.

"No, that's bullshit. There's nothing free about love. It comes at a really high price. It's a heartbreaking motherfucker," she says. Her nonchalance is infuriating. "But that..." She nods toward the bed. "That's something else. Like he said, it just comes with the territory."

"Good for you that you can talk yourself into believing that," I say. She rummages in the sheets for the missing earring. I feel a lecture coming on—from me, that is. It's probably meant for Jimmy, but she's the only one here.

"I'm all for sex positivity and minding your own business," I begin. "Other people's expectations…who needs 'em? If you can make some sort of situationship work for you, go you. But sooner or later, and you can quote me on this, someone's going to wake up one morning, roll over and say, 'Guess what, I want you all to myself. I didn't think I would but as it turns out, I do. Actually, I'm besotted with you.' And just like that, the rules of this game? Broken—I know, I know—by definition, free love has no rules, so all bets are off rule-wise. But chances are that leaves you, the rolling-over person, lying here next to a big, fat empty…I don't know what…just empty. Just because you suddenly wanted…make that needed…needed in a way you didn't see coming…the 'C' word…commitment. And then you know what happens? All the ideology falls away. And you're left with…FWB."

She stares at me blankly.

"Friends with benefits. The no-idealism, all-pragmatism, sad little step-cousin of…" I gesture toward the bed with a grand sweep of the hand, "…this."

I keep going. "I know girls who can pull it off. My best friend, Sarah…she has a whole spiel about her busy life and how she doesn't have the time or the room for a relationship. But that's not me. Never has been. Probably my problem, I'm not going to lie." I breathe. "I'm sorry. I'm not mad at you."

"I know," she says. She pulls on her knee-high moccasin boots. They actually look sexy on her which is simply no fair. If I wore those things, I'd look like I was in a school pageant about the first Thanksgiving.

She pauses at the door on her way out. "Don't hold this against Jimmy," she says. Then she's gone.

Alone in Jimmy's room, I smooth out the sheets. There's her earring buried inside a fold. I lay the oversized gold hoop on the pillow—a totem. My jeans and sweater are still tied in the bundle from the thrift store. I can't untie the knot in the twine. I try and try but cannot. I bite the inside of my cheek to dam the tears.

My eyes land on the silly child's desk in the corner. I lift the top. It's full of little kid supplies, like it was never stripped of its original incarnation. I grab the small, rounded scissors and have at the twine. They're kiddie-safe, not at all sharp, but I manage to saw through.

I quickly change into my real clothes. The one-dollar strand of love beads falls off when I pull the dress over my head. I lay the hippie dress on the bed and toss the beads on top of it. There's some symbolism there in the dress laid out on Jimmy's bed, but…it escapes me. Zero synapses firing.

He did that.

I stare at the dress a moment longer. It's painfully obvious. I don't belong here. This is not my time.

I grab my camera and head downstairs.

The smell of stale smoke—cigarettes and weed—hangs in the foyer. I glance into the parlor. Royce isn't there anymore, just the random hangers-on asleep on the sofa. Wine bottles and beer cans clutter every surface. A few pieces of cast-off clothing are scattered around. Record albums lie here and there, apart from their covers. A red wine stain has spread across the seat of my favorite wing chair. Do I have a minute to hunt for some club soda to get rid of the splotch? Is club soda the best thing? The instinct to google sends my hand grabbing for my phone in my back pocket. I find only tush.

I duck into the powder room and lock the door behind me. My heart pounds like I'm stealing the Hope Diamond. I open the little cupboard and reach behind all the never-to-be-used cans and sprays and pull out the box of S.O.S. I open the box and carefully reach for my phone, like touching one of those scrubby pads will set off an alarm, like I'm playing that game Operation. I extract my phone and slip it into my back pocket. The weight of it there sends me back, a weird sensorial time travel.

I close the cupboard quietly, catching a glimpse of myself in the mirror. I lean in closer. There it is. The groove. I run my finger between my eyebrows. It wasn't there when I was seventeen. I can't really see it now but I feel it…a little. I'm exhausted. My face turns into a Magic Eye poster. I can look through the face in the mirror to my thirty-four-year-old face. Then it disappears.

I tiptoe into the foyer, passing the parlor on the right, passing the dining room on the left.

Jimmy and Royce are staked out in there—the whir of the tape recorder the only sound.

CHAPTER ELEVEN

I BOUND UP THE stairs to Vic's apartment. On my previous visit to 1967, I had no idea how I was going to get home, if I was going to get home. It's different this time. I suspect Vic's darkroom is the portal, or at least *a* portal. Last time, it got complicated. I tried to reverse engineer my hurdle through time. I replayed the steps that got me here: the van and the bridge…the van and the bridge. But it turned out to be a hat trick: the van, the bridge, and the rain. Not to mention a bump on the head, that pesky element that's itched my brain ever since, making me wonder if the whole thing really happened or was nothing more than a post-traumatic hallucination. (As noted, I've done my research.) I'm older now; I have a less precarious relationship with reality. Theoretically. I'm pretty sure I'm here. So, once again…how do I get back? That leads me to the darkroom.

I arrive at the top of the rickety stairs, having lost all track of time. You don't show up at someone's door when it's still pre-dawn dark. Yet, here I am at Vic's door. I test the doorknob. It turns. I wonder if I'll find the Amazon pick-up office—sterile and plastic—or Vic's apartment. Is this apartment a wrinkle in time that's different on any given day, depending on how the universe folds itself, like origami? A fish one day, a butterfly the next? A lotus? A crane? I open the door slowly, wincing against the creak.

My eyes fall on Vic's battered tea kettle, then his wacky collection of cookie jars: the owl, the piglet, the Aunt Jemima that would so get him so canceled. I exhale. I didn't realize how much I was hoping it would be Vic's home and not the Amazon office.

I tiptoe into the living room expecting to find Vic asleep on the pull-out couch. The couch is opened into a bed. The bed is disheveled, but Vic's not in it. My heart lurches. Is he okay? I scan the room. The red light is on over the darkroom door. He must go in there when he can't sleep. He sure is my grandfather. Insomnia may be genetic but coping with insomnia by developing photographs—that's more than genetic. That's magic.

I approach the door, tripping over Tripod, his three-legged cat. The cat lets out a yowl. "Sorry," I say.

"Who's there?" says Vic from behind the door.

"It's just me," I say, moving closer to the door. "I'm so sorry. I tripped over Tripod."

"Mari?"

"Yes, sorry, it's me. Mari."

"You remembered his name."

"Of course. Tripod!"

"I can't open the door right now," says Vic from his side. "Are you okay? What's wrong?"

"Nothing."

"Don't bullshit a bullshitter."

"You don't strike me as a bullshitter."

"See there," he says, "obviously I'm not a very good one."

I drop to the floor near the door and sit facing it. "I'm not sure where I belong."

I hear the swish of paper through the soup. "Nobody's sure at your age."

I lean my forehead against the door.

"Just a few more minutes," he says. "Almost done."

"I don't want to interrupt you," I say. I hear him drop something, his tongs probably. He groans to bend and pick them up. "I know how you have to strike while the creative spark is hot. Not the best metaphor, given the history of flammable photographic chemicals and all…"

"Don't worry about it, honey."

"Worrying is my hobby," I say. "Although, come to think of it, not so much since I've been here."

"Then maybe it turns out here is where you belong."

I lift my head from the door and sit at attention, ready for guidance. "You think?"

"I don't know," he says. "Something to consider." I hear more sloshing. "As long as your folks know where you are. Dollars to doughnuts you learned worrying from them and you don't want them worried sick about you."

"I think they're over worrying about me."

I study the black-and-white photograph hanging on the wall beside the door—a photo Vic took—my father as a little boy. I remember the moment it dawned on me. That's my father. Vic is my grandfather. That kind of psychic jolt permanently alters your DNA. I raise the Leica to my eye and take a picture of the picture. Click.

One more. But no Click. End of the roll.

I rewind the film, listening for that satisfying ratchet, then flip open the back of the camera and remove the cartridge. "Can I leave a roll of film for you to develop?"

"Sure thing," he says.

"I'll put it here on the table."

I pick up a new roll in its little orange box and load it in. "I'm taking a new roll too, if that's okay?"

"I'll put it on your tab," he chuckles.

I place the exposed roll next to the TV Guide on the coffee table. The caption tells me the guy on the cover is Raymond Burr of *Ironside*. Never heard of him, never heard of the show. Across the top of the Guide: "Do TV Cameras Add To Riot Flames?" Good question. I guess some questions never get answered.

"Kiddo, you still there?" he asks from the other side of the door.

"I'm here."

"Just so you know—parents are never done worrying about their kids. That I promise you."

My hand flies to the locket pressed against my chest beneath my sweater. I can't imagine a time when I won't worry about Joni.

"But what do I know?" he says from his side of the door. "I'm just a dad. The world is built on mothers."

I turn back to the darkroom door. "I'm so glad I found you."

"Glad to know you, too," he says. "I'm always here. Whenever you need me."

I smile at my own little secret. "Thank you," I say, then head back through the kitchen, down the stairs, and out into the haze.

I'm pretty sure the darkroom is a piece of the portal puzzle. But it's occupied. I'll have to wait.

Down the street, newspapers are being stocked in front of the Pall Mall Lounge. Inside, the counter boy is making a fresh pot of coffee. He's the pudgy ten-year-old with a white-blond bowl-cut. The bell over the door jingles as I enter. The kid slides a cup of coffee in front of me as soon as my butt hits the stool.

"Hi," I say. "I remember you."

"Sorry," he says. "A lot of people come in and out of here."

"Sure. I didn't expect you to…You gave me a hamburger for free once. A long time ago…you know, like over the summer."

"Cream?" he asks.

"Please." He places the miniature ribbed glass pitcher in front of me.

"Don't you go to school?" I ask.

"Not like real school."

"You're homeschooled?"

He shrugs. "It's called unschooled."

"That's a new one… So you're like in the un-fifth grade?"

"Fourth… I think."

He takes a blueberry muffin from under a glass dome, places it on a plate, and sets it in front of me. "On the house."

"Thanks," I say. I rip off a piece. It's at least a couple days old, but it feels good to put something in my stomach. "So…unschooling. Like unlearning all the nonsense that society has drummed into us?"

"I guess," he says, topping off my coffee. "More like what they call child-led learning. I'm the child. That's me."

"That's you."

"And learning through experiences in life." He's got the pitch down.

"That's this." I open my two hands and swing them wide to indicate the diner.

"They say it strengthens family bonds." He nods toward the short order cook on the other side of the pass-through window.

"Your dad?'

Counter Boy nods.

I wave to his father. He smiles at me.

"How about your mom?"

"She's gone."

"I'm sorry."

"Not dead or anything. She went to live in Vermont to do organic farming. Do you know what that is?"

"I do," I say.

I stop myself from asking if he misses her. Of course he misses her. She's his mother. The world is built on mothers.

The bell over the door jingles.

"There you are." Nina's voice, unmistakably smokey. She strides in and settles onto the stool next to me. Mussed hair, yesterday's black eyeliner smudged. She hasn't slept. "I never thought I'd say this, but I've been looking for you."

"Why?"

Counter Boy pours her a cup of coffee. "Cream?"

"Black," she says. No softening any edges for Nina. She barely looks at me, but she couldn't be more direct. "You've got to come back."

"Where?"

"To the house," she says. She pounds back the coffee. "You want me to spell it out? Fine. I'll spell it out. Jimmy's hung up on you. Or thinks he is."

"Last time, you told me that if he loved me, I had to break his heart, that he could only write when he was heartbroken. Blah, blah, blah." (This girl brings out the blah, blah, blah in me. Besides, all those fifty-cent words don't feel so impressive anymore; they just feel like trying too hard.)

"That was then, this is now," says Nina.

"Easy for you to say."

"Things are different. This is real life."

"I reiterate. Easy for you to say."

"Stop being cute," says Nina. She gestures at Counter Boy for a refill. "When you were here last time…" she trails off. "It doesn't matter. It was a different world for the band. We've got a fuckin' hit record now. And a contract. We can't wait around for the boy wonder to be touched by his muse. He's got to spit out some songs for an album. Like now."

"You sound like Royce."

"I don't give a shit about Royce." she spits out. "It's Jimmy. He'll be miserable if he fucks up this chance. He'll regret it for the rest of his life. I know him."

"So *you* talk to him," I say.

She shakes her head. "It's got to be you, my little pretty. You've got to light a fire under him."

"He doesn't care about me," I say. "He was in bed with that girl…"

Nina waves dismissively. "That doesn't mean anything."

"I'm sick of people telling me that. I'm allowed to say what means something. If it means something to me, it means something." I brace for it.

"You're right," says Nina.

"I am?" Shock of the year—whichever year: Nina agreeing with me.

Nina stares into her coffee. "Listen, the band is like a family. If you want to be with Jimmy, and he wants to be with you, then you're part of the family, like it or not. I may not like it, but it seems out of my control."

I stare at her. I thought that was the one thing we had in common: control at all costs. (That, and Jimmy.)

"Anyway," she goes on. "Being part of the family means thinking about what's good for everyone."

"Including you."

"Oh, there's no getting rid of me. Jimmy and I are on this long, strange trip together. Wherever that takes us, whatever that means. Meanwhile, you get your ass back there and make nice. For the good of the band." She slams a quarter onto the counter and swivels off her stool. "You'll figure it out," she says. She downs the last of her coffee and strides out. "You're not as dumb as you look."

My jaw clenches. She's so exasperating.

"You're so extra!" I call after her.

She turns to look at me.

"Like, making your parents go to Magnolia Thunderpussy!" I elaborate— loudly. "I mean, who does that?"

Nina shakes her head like I'm a crazy person and strides out.

All eyes on me…all two patrons. Including the guy in the back booth. It's Bodhi, a couple of hefty law books splayed open in front of him. He waves me over.

"I thought that was you," he says. "What brings you here at this hour?"

"Long story," I say. "And you?'

"Midterms. Been here since Frizzie's."

"Yikes," I say. "Good for you, though…for sticking with it."

"Bizarrely," he considers, "it gives me hope."

"Hope?" I say. "School gives you hope? I thought this whole thing—movement, era, whatevs—was about hope. Experimenting with…I don't know…lifestyles, I guess, for lack of a less generic, antiseptic, fundamentally meaningless word. I thought it was all a massive act of hope. For a better…everything? So you're saying, you channel all your hope into this?" I rest my hand on the fattest book like I'm taking an oath.

"Yeah," he says, slipping a bookmark in and closing the book. "I know it's not cool, but sometimes I feel like what I'm learning about is the only hope. There's a reason they say 'the law of the land.' If we can change the laws, we can change the land."

I'm flooded with all the ways his conviction is going to be betrayed, all the ways cynicism and self-interest and gazillionaires will elbow out hope. I could blast him with that litany. But why would I? I envy his hopefulness.

Bodhi slides me his plate with a leftover piece of bacon, then gathers his books and papers into his satchel. Under the law tomes lies an oversized paperback: *The Family of Man*. The cover features a collage of brightly colored rectangles. A young face smiles from the black-and-white photo in the center—gender and nationality indeterminate. I guess that's the point. Someone simply belonging to the family of man. They're playing some sort of primitive flute.

I pick up the book. "Tax law, I presume?" I joke.

I leaf through it, landing on a photo of a couple kissing on the street with all this hustle and bustle around them.

He laughs. "I always bring a picture book along for when all the words in these…" He taps his satchel. "…Start going fuzzy and don't make any sense."

"Smart. Photography's kind of my thing."

"I figured," he says, nodding toward my Leica.

"I wanted to be a rock 'n' roll photographer. Album covers. *Rolling Stone* magazine…"

"Don't know it," he says.

"Wow," I say. "You will."

"You're shooting Neon Dream, right?" he says, encouraging. "That'll get your name out there."

"It's too late," I say.

"Not right this minute." He thinks I'm talking time-of-day when I'm really talking time-of-life.

I keep paging through. Faces of people from all over the world. "I guess it's easier to have a kumbaya moment with the quote-unquote family of man than with actual people, not to mention your own dysfunctional family."

Bodhi nods. "I can dig that."

I slide the photography book back to him.

"You can hang onto it if you like," he says. "For inspiration…"

"Thanks," I say, "but that's okay…"

He picks up the book of photographs. "Mari," he says, slipping the book into his satchel, "you can do whatever you like. Take back your dream."

What I don't say out loud is how much Jimmy is a part of that dream. He has been for half my life… Maybe he can be for the rest of it.

CHAPTER TWELVE

I head home through the sunrise streets—scratch that. No matter what bogus spin Nina put on the whole "family" situation, the Victorian's not home. Not as long as Nina's around. And she's made it perfectly clear, she's not going anywhere.

As long as Jimmy's here, she's here.

As long as Jimmy's here…

Right there, it occurs to me. Right there in front of the shuttered Psychedelic Shop. A genuine aha moment. Bodhi was right. I *can* take back my dream. Literally. I'll take Jimmy back with me…to my time.

I race to the Victorian. Royce is in the parlor, half-asleep over a cup of coffee. P.J. and Sam wander in right after me, arriving home after an all-nighter of who-knows-what. They flop onto the couch.

I head upstairs but stop halfway and dash back down. I plant myself in front of Royce.

"I know you sent me up to Jimmy's room so I'd find him with that girl. For all I know, you sent her up to his room just so you could send me up there to find them together."

His eyes widen. Bingo.

"Of course you did," I say. "That's exactly how you operate. And that's exactly what you are. An operator. You are so ahead of your time, so not of this time. Like me. But I'm going to fix that. For me, not for you. You're going to have to wait it out. I told you…your time is out there, and it's not a pretty picture. Now, it's all about the music. The Dead have a house and the Airplane have a house. And Janis. And you guys have this house. You know what they're going to be replaced with? Hacker houses, where people build start-ups and develop AI."

"AI?" says Sam, perking up.

"Artificial intelligence," I say.

"Is there any other kind?" Sam wonders.

"You're headed for a doom loop," I say.

"That could be a song," says P.J.

"It's more than a song," I say, chomping the scenery. "It's an anthem." I face Royce. "For people just like you. You'll see."

I point a finger at Royce. "I'm over the whole Jimmy with another girl thing. Cheap trick on your part. Stupid young guy thing on Jimmy's part. He is young. I forget that. Groupies come with the rock star territory. Stupid comes with the young territory." I fix him with a stare. "But chaos comes with the greed territory."

I turn on my heels and head upstairs. Nina sits, knees to chest, on the landing in a long silk kimono. She does a slow clap.

"You heard?" I say.

"I did."

"So…" I say, "I'll be the grown-up. I forgive him."

She scoots against the wall, giving me room to pass. "Thank you," she says. It could be the first time she's ever uttered the words.

I pause on the step above her. "You never give up," I say, not turning to see her face.

"No."

I nod. "That's a good thing."

The sounds of false starts filter from Jimmy's room. I knock. No response. I crack the door. He's stretched out on the bed leaning against the wall, half on top of the hippie dress still laid there, resting his forehead against the guitar in his hands. I venture in.

"I'm sorry," he says, looking up. A cassette recorder sits next to him on the bed.

"I know."

"'Nuff said." We say it simultaneously.

He lays the guitar on the floor, stands and crosses to me. I slip the Leica off my neck and set it on the child's desk in the corner. Jimmy wraps his arms around me, cradling the back of my head with one hand, pulling me close against his chest.

"I love you," he says.

"I know. You love me so much."

He holds me tighter. "It's important that you know that."

"I do," I say. "We know that about each other."

He kisses me. And we meet somewhere between our times, outside of time.

"Would you come home with me?" I ask.

"I'll go anywhere with you."

He kisses me again. I can't let myself get lost in this kiss. I have to make sure this will work.

"Anywhere could be stranger than you think," I say. "Like, really different."

"How different could it be?"

I search his eyes. For one thing, I'll be thirty-four. Also known as: twelve years older than you. That's pretty different. Will he want me then? I sweep away the image of our age-gap selves. Besides, the May-December thing is kind of having a moment. And we'd be more like July-November anyway.

"You like adventure, right? New places?" I hope.

"As long as I can make music... What do you think of this?" He steps to the bed, presses PLAY on the tape recorder. "Just messing around with something..."

No words, just music. So pretty. The phrase repeats, a shift in key. Major to minor? More melancholy. A long, lingering note.

"I love it," I say. "Lyrics?"

"Words'll come. I need to get out, listen to the city... I got a good start on another song, too...about the other day...called *Fortune Cookie*. Royce hated the title," he almost chuckles. "Not commercial enough."

"He's clueless."

Beyond true. Even Royce has no clue what commercial really means. Likes, stans, and downloads. Videos and merch, sampling and autotune, streaming and digital sales. Can I picture Jimmy living in that world? Thriving?

Of course. Why not? So many ways to get music out there. What's not to love?

"Wouldn't it be awesome if you had a device in your pocket that had every song in the world? And you could listen to whatever you wanted whenever you wanted. Any song. A whole cloudful of songs. You could find any song, any artist, instantly. And listen wherever you are with just these tiny little earbuds…itty bitty headphones that fit into your ears. You can't even see them. So, like, everybody walking down the street could be listening to their own thing. Doesn't that sound amazing?"

He considers a moment. Then shakes his head. "The opposite."

"I'm not explaining it well. You wouldn't have to have a radio or a stereo. No going to the record store."

"I love the record store," he says.

"Any song you like playing right there in your own ears."

"Sounds kind of…isolating."

"But the cool part—" Suddenly, I've forgotten what the cool part is.

"Music's for sharing, right?" he says. "Like when we heard 'Moonlight'…that day in the park…or when we were all in the backyard and it came on the radio… It was magic."

Jimmy will bring the magic with him.

"But you can make music anywhere, right?"

He shrugs.

Of course he can make music anywhere…

But maybe not anytime.

There's no separating Jimmy from his music. But is his music part of his time? Is that what makes it timeless?

I'm overthinking. He'll love it there. Like a vacation. Even if he doesn't know it starts with a walk to Vic's camera store.

"We'll be back in time to cut the album, right?" he says. The tape recorder clicks, then a whirring as the tape winds itself out. Jimmy leans over to press STOP.

Wait. Is Neon Dream a one-hit wonder because of me? Because I dragged him away?

I don't know how any of this works. I only know I want to be with Jimmy. I've taken a long and winding road to get here, but I've finally figured out there's a halfway decent version of me, a version I can actually live with. It's the one right here, right now... with Jimmy.

He does that.

But he does that because he's here. And now.

I shuffle through all the ways to make sense of bringing Jimmy home with me, all the ways to make it work.

There are none.

Jimmy can only be himself in this time and place. And I don't want to change him.

But I can't stay.

With Jimmy, I'm a me without the brain clutter, a me who can silence this exhausting inner chatter. But I'm not whole here.

My chest squeezes. The press of tears hits hard.

"What is it?" Jimmy asks.

I shake my head. "My heart..."

He looks at me like maybe I'm having a heart attack.

I place a hand on my heart to contain its beating. "It's like it's too full."

Jimmy wraps his arms around me and holds me close so that the solidity of his chest calms the flutter in mine.

I let him go once before. I can do it again. I will do it to be—

Aha moment 2.0.

"I have to go do something," I say. "I'm not sure how long it'll take. But I'll be back."

"You're leaving again."

"Only for a little while...I think. I'll do my best to make sure it's a very little while."

"That's what you said last time."

"This is different. This time I know where everyone belongs." I pick up the Leica and hand it to him. "And because I'm going to leave this with you. You know I'll always come back for that."

"I'll take runner-up to a camera if I have to." He half-smiles, one eyebrow raised.

"You don't have to. You're not runner-up to anyone," I say. "Besides, you won't have time to miss me. You're going to be so busy writing songs. Listen to me, I know you have them in you. That's your magic. You're meant to be a songwriter."

"You really believe that?"

"I really do."

"I really believe in you, too."

"We're going to have a whole new life when I come back," I say.

I pull his face down to mine and kiss him. "We're going to be what we're supposed to be." I rest my head against his chest again. I'm not sure how I'm going to explain Joni to him, but I'll find a way.

IN A FLASH, I'M dashing through the busy streets toward the camera shop. Pounding the pavement on a mission to rescue Joni from so much peril. From social isolation and social media. From deepfakes and the dark web. From cunning viruses and species extinction. From cheat codes and cyberbullying. From extreme weather and digital addiction. From culture wars and identity theft. From quiet quitting and zoom fatigue. From apps and thirst traps. From CGI and IRL, NFTs and iOS. From misinformation and disinformation and at-all-cost formation of us-against-them. I need to get her back here, hook her up to the IV of hope that is the sixties. Hope and imagination—the purview of the young.

I take the rickety stairs two by two and dart into Vic's kitchen. It's still his kitchen. Vic is asleep on the couch. No need to wake him to say goodbye. I'll be back soon enough. I can't wait for him to meet his great-granddaughter. It might be time to tell him the whole crazy story. I suspect he'd believe it.

I tiptoe into the darkroom and close the door.

I flick the switch that turns on the red light outside. I breathe deep, summoning all the time travel mojo I possibly can.

Photos hang clipped to the line strung across the room from hook to hook. They're mine. Vic developed the roll of film I left behind. I want to thank him.

There's an old-fashioned typewriter on top of an old-fashioned file cabinet in the corner. A stack of blank paper lies next to it. I feed a sheet into the roller. I've seen secretaries using these things on *Mad Men*, of course, but I've never laid hands on one myself. I fumble until I lift the metal bar off the roller to get the paper in right. The paper isn't perfectly straight, but who cares. Vic won't.

I type. The keys make a sharp clack. They're crazy loud and I worry I might wake him.

Dear Vic,

Thank you for everything.
See you soon.

Love,
Mari

It's a feeble note. There's so much more I want to say. I consider ripping the paper out and starting over, but time is of the essence and I'm not sure I'd do better on a second try. I want to tell him that he's my grandfather and that I love him, but I can't do that. Certainly not yet. I like to think he feels the familial tug between us without my having to put it into words. But I'm not the best at reading other people's feelings, especially about me. Just ask Nathan.

I leave the page in the typewriter.

I study the photos on the line, images of the last few days dangling in front of me. From the backseat of the limo: hippies snatching up giveaways at the Psychedelic Shop; Neon Dream on the dais at the press conference in the fancy hotel; a young Mr. Chappell at Sam Wo's holding his chopstick aloft; the charred coffin planks sticking out of a garbage can; the ethereal folk duo at Frizzie's closing night; my dad as a kid in the black-and-white photograph on his father's wall, Vic's wall. And Jimmy. So many shots of Jimmy—Jimmy at the press conference; Jimmy holding the 45 of his song; the selfie of me and Jimmy reflected in the shop window. Hanging next to that shot is a close-up of my locket. Vic must have cropped it from the selfie and blown it up.

I slip my phone out of my back pocket to take a picture of that picture. It's easy enough to take a close-up of the locket any time I like, but I want this exact picture of this exact way Vic saw something in the original.

My phone is dead, the screen completely black. Obviously. Duh. I have to go *through* the portal. And then what?

Last time, I had to cross the bridge. Maybe this time it's a different kind of structure. Not a bridge, but the stairs. Probably not the rickety back stairs which seem entrenched in '67, but the front stairs, the interior staircase that leads directly into the Amazon pick-up center. My heart beats harder. There's a poetic sense to this theory that feels right. Back stairs take you back. Front stairs take you forward.

I tiptoe out of the darkroom. Vic still snores on the couch. Tripod the cat is curled at the top of his head like a fur hat. I creep through the room and inch open the front door. That staircase is sturdy and unsplintered, nothing like the back stairs. Surely it must be the bullet train to the future.

I wince against the first few steps, hoping they won't creak. Then I charge down the rest, clutching my phone, pressing the power button for it to flash on. It doesn't. I press it again. And again. Nothing.

The last stair deposits me in Vic's camera store. Not an Amazon sign in sight. My chest constricts. My temples pound. Sweat beads at the back of my neck. Panic.

My phone is still dead. Of course it is. It's a cell phone in 1967. I'm stuck. So stuck. What if my real life was a hallucination? Maybe I am a child of the sixties for real. Maybe I did some bad drugs and a string of synapses misfired so radically that the dream seemed like reality and reality seemed like the dream. If Haight-Ashbury, 1967 is my true reality, then Joni doesn't exist.

I dig my locket out from under my sweater. I'm trembling too much to wedge my thumbnail into the groove. Finally, I manage to pry open the heart. I close my eyes, willing Joni into existence. I open my eyes. There she is. Her little face, more than half her life ago, but still her—so essentially her. In her eyes: the wonder that has shined since the moment she was born. Joni exists. And if Joni exists, that reality wins. No contest.

But she is there.

And I am here.

I've got to get back.

Back stairs, back to the future…back stairs, back to the future… I bound up the front stairs, but tiptoe through Vic's time-worn apartment to the kitchen, to the back door. With all due respect to Marty McFly, I repeat the phrase in my head, a mantra, willing it to be true. *Back stairs, back to the future…back stairs, back to the future…* I escape to the top step and turn my phone over in my hand like a magician revealing a card. Black screen. I force myself to breathe as I descend a step and reboot. I pray the words as I perform the functions.

Press the side button—

Drag the slider—

Press the side button—

I hold the side button, ticking off the seconds with each descending step. One—one thousand, two—one thousand. Suddenly, I'm all about mantras. Something, anything, to keep me focused instead of spinning out of control…

Joni's going to think I've abandoned her. For the past many months, I've been so preoccupied with her growing up in a broken home that I neglected to recognize that a broken home is still some sort of home. I conjure her little face, eyes wide with confusion and disbelief, when she realizes I'm not there…and then, after however long it takes, for her to realize that I'm never going to be there. Her mother's not coming back.

Three—one thousand. I give myself an extra second. Four—one thousand.

I hold my breath from the last step to the pavement…and release the button. There it is in the middle of the screen: the apple. Connection. It fades in, glowing silver, its halo growing brighter and brighter. I'm back.

All around me is a gentrified Haight. Upscale this, gourmet that, renovated everything.

I rush to my car, praying it hasn't been towed. Windshield papered with tickets—who cares. Just let the car be there. I fly by shop window after shop window—wacky socks, bizarre toys. A yellow plush Bert or Ernie wannabe holds a sign, "Don't hug me. I'm scared." Too big a hurry to stop for a present for Joni. She doesn't need another toy. She needs me.

I break into a run. A mural blurs by. I veer past a statue of a robot, shiny silver and rigid. It jerks to life. Guy's got to make a living. No time to tip him.

I weave through a clump of women dressed in athleisure carrying yoga mats. The Haight's version of my Marin County girly-girls.

I pray my car is in the next block. A driver leans on his horn as I dash across the street against the light. Sweat pricks my forehead. My quads burn. But I could run all the way across the bridge if I had to.

Is it this block? No.

Heart pumping for a last push. I zag through cars stopped at a red.

Which direction to run?

Where's the Amoeba sign?

That way.

There's my car. No mistaking my CR-V—the hefty dent in the fender I haven't had time to get fixed. I slide my key fob from the pocket of my phone case and click to open. I see the car's taillights flash orange as the car unlocks. A few more jogs and I'm there. Only one ticket on the windshield. I slide behind the wheel and start the car. I allow myself one deep breath, flicking on my turn signal…tick, tick. It's then, during that breath, that I glance into the rearview mirror. Something's weird.

I turn around and study the back seat. Something's definitely weird. Like one of those hidden picture games. Where the hell is Waldo? No, it's not like that. Nothing is hidden. Something is missing. Joni's car seat.

My hands go clammy. My stomach loops-the-loop. My brain zigzags every which way. No explanation. Actually, only one. No car seat, no Joni. Joni was never born.

I open the photo app on my phone and stare at the grid of tiny thumbnail photos. I go to *Albums*. No Joni album. I do a search for Joni. Nothing. I should have noticed: her face didn't fill the screen after the phone powered up. I did something on this trip that short-circuited my whole life. Or at least the most important part, the Joni part.

My mind pinballs madly, trying to figure out what I did. Tick, tick.

The Spice Girls sing. *"Mama, my friend…"*

I answer the phone. "Mom?"

"What's wrong?" Moms can do that—know instantly when something's wrong.

My breathing comes in tiny, desperate slurps.

"Nothing," I manage. "Just tired." *Please ask about Joni…please ask about Joni…*

"I got a new listing," she says. "Whoever thought we could ask one-point-nine in the Haight?"

"Wow." *Ask about Joni…ask about Joni…*

"I know, right?"

"Right," I say.

She keeps talking as I turn around and stare into the back seat to make sure my eyes weren't playing a trick. Maybe I missed it. Maybe I missed the big hulking car seat that took the expert from Baby Gear twenty minutes to install. It's not there. Definitely.

Instead, there's a manila envelope. I reach back and grab it. A proof sheet peeks out. I slide it out. Shot after shot of Imagine Dragons in concert. High shutter speed captures them frozen in motion. High ISO, too, just high enough to cope with low light, but not too high to increase the image noise. These are real-deal, you-are-there concert photos.

Something else back there, too. I pick it up. A backstage pass hanging from a lanyard. With Tamara Caldwell on it. Whoa. I took these photos. Tick, tick.

My mom says something. I have no idea what. Then, "Mari? Are you sure you're okay?"

"Have you spoken to Joni?"

"Joni?" *She's not being funny.*

My throat constricts.

"Joni who?" she says.

"Trying to remember…someone's name…someone who…"

"I don't remember a Joni," she says. "From the neighborhood?"

"Might have been," I sputter.

I throw open the car door and vomit into the street.

CHAPTER THIRTEEN

THE VICTORIAN IS QUIET when I creep in. Gulping for air. I made it…somehow. Somehow it all worked. My rewind back to '67. Upstairs, darkroom, down the back, through the Haight, running straight here like a shot. Running…running to reset, reboot, re-whatever went haywire.

I head up to Jimmy's room. Who cares if Jade Eyes or some other groupie is in his bed? I can feel no deeper emptiness. I'm only going in to get my camera.

After mentally tracing the steps of the whole portal moment, it's all I can come up with. My camera. It might be the extra element required to transport me back to the proper future, the one that stars Joni. Who knows? Not me. I'm on a scavenger hunt without a list of items to be found.

I sneak in. Jimmy's alone, asleep. The camera is there on the little desk. I run my fingers over its pebbly surface. Every time I've held it in my hands, every time I've clicked the shutter is etched there in that surface. I thought I had to leave it here. Like last time. But everything was different then. I had all the time in the world to trust that the camera would find its way to me.

That was before Joni.

Joni changed everything.

Different times, different rules for sliding between them. I don't exactly know what those rules are, but what did being so sure of the rules ever do for me anyway? I used to care, but times have changed. It's up to me to carry forward the Leica's history. No matter how the whole time travel thing worked last time, I'm not leaving without my camera this time.

I look through the viewfinder at Jimmy lying on the bed, his leg stretched across my hippie dress.

I can't just disappear out of his life like I did when I was here before. When I really was seventeen. Especially since I promised him I'd be back.

I lie down next to him and rest a hand on his bare chest. I stare at his face. Part of me is waiting for the whoosh of longing that always sparks when I touch him. But there's too much in the way. Too many years in too many directions. And the gaping hole in all those years. Joni's absence. I'm suddenly so much older than Jimmy. I should have been old enough to know better.

Joni refers to all past as "yesterday" and all future as "tomorrow." To her, both yesterday and tomorrow are so far away from "now" that you might as well lump them all together. All yesterday stretches backward, all tomorrow stretches forward. She's so much smarter than I am. I got greedy and wanted all the times—yesterday, today, and tomorrow—all at once.

I bend closer to Jimmy and breathe in his scent. No wonder I wanted to stay here. I thought I could build a life here with Jimmy. I thought I could keep his creative spark lit and maybe even change his course from one-hit wonder to star. I pretended I could fold Joni into that vison. The three of us would live a perfect peace-and-love life. But she doesn't belong here.

And there's no peace and no love if there's no Joni. There's nothing if there's no Joni.

My brain buzzes with half-assed explanations and half-laid plans, like Jimmy's half-written songs. I struggle to still my heart hammering against my ribs. I study Jimmy's face where my own private calm used to live. What I see there now is the face of my old love…my real life old love. James. Jimmy's son. I see James's face in his father's.

James looks so much like his father. The same plane from cheekbone to jaw, the same mink eyelashes, the slightest cleft in the chin. But with his mother's eyes. Nina's eyes.

I'm so stupid. There would be no James if Jimmy and I stayed together. And the world needs James. He's one of the good guys. Of course he is. He's Jimmy's son. Since splitting with Nathan, I've thought a lot about why James and I broke up. I haven't figured anything out, just done a lot of thinking. Like all breakups, my breakup with James was complicated. He sensed something troubled me about being with him, something I couldn't articulate. Girl dates man, then girl dates his son. It happens. But girl leapfrogs over four decades to do so…while remaining seventeen? Not simply hard to articulate. Impossible to believe.

I convinced myself that James and I were not meant to be.

Jimmy and Nina. They're meant to be. There's no room for me in that equation. I knew that the last time I was here. I got behind the wheel of that crazy painted van and drove across the bridge, sweaty palms and all, to find Nina in Sausalito and drag her back to The Fillmore. I knew she had to sing with the band that night. It was the only way Neon Dream could win the Battle of the Bands. I told myself that's why I kidnapped her from her waitress job and delivered her to Jimmy. But part of me knew that I was not just delivering her voice—the thing that made Neon Dream special. I was delivering *her* to Jimmy.

That detour to 1967 had cracked open my hard candy shell, the shell I'd spent my young life cultivating. For once, I wanted what someone else wanted. I wanted what Jimmy wanted, which was to have a hit record with the band he'd put together with a song he'd written. That was the most important part—the song. Jimmy wanted to be heard. Nina knew that about him. That's why she was perfect for him. And that was why, no matter her trying everything in her formidable power to get rid of me, I finally got rid of myself.

I uncurl myself from Jimmy's side and sit up. I love this room. The silly child's desk with the seat attached from a time even before this time. The overstuffed easy chair in the corner. The yellow glass lamp etched with flowers and its cracked faux-Tiffany shade. The nubby chenille bedspread. The fine coat of dust settled everywhere. And the young man sleeping there. Very young. Too young for the real me.

I can't fill in the blanks for him like his life were a paint-by-the-numbers kit. It's enough that I inspired his first great song. He can take it from here.

I kiss his cheek. His eyes open in slo-mo. "You're back already?" he says.

"I haven't left."

"Good," he says. "So you didn't mean goodbye?"

And then it hits me. I didn't then, but I do now. Maybe I need to say a real goodbye. Not the mid-point of a round-trip goodbye. Goodbye to more than just Jimmy, but to that seventeen-year-old notion that Jimmy is The One. I've been walking around with that notion for literally half my life. There's a good chance it warped my time with James, warped my marriage to Nathan, like a vinyl record album left too long in the sun. You know there's music embedded in the thing, but you can't play it.

"I mean it now," I say.

He furrows his brow and takes hold of my hand. "Can you stay a little longer? Just till morning?"

"It is morning," I say.

"Wow!" he says. "How did that happen?"

I smile. "It has something to do with the sun and the moon and how the earth turns."

"How the earth turns…" he repeats.

Jimmy watches me slip the camera over my head. My heart races. Butterflies flutter in my stomach.

All I know is erasing Joni dialed down my lust for this era. I no longer feel free and gloriously irresponsible. Maybe I toyed with (a.k.a. fucked with) the space-time matrix so cavalierly that I had to pay. You always have to pay. This time the price is too high.

I perch on the edge of the bed. "You know what I said about how you're the one…?"

"Yeah…?" he says. "You want to take that back?"

"No. No, not at all." I lace my fingers through his. "Only that I think maybe the idea of there being one person for each of us…"

Jimmy scoots up on the bed, his back now upright against the wall.

"I'm saying…" What am I saying? "I'm saying maybe there's room for more than one only one…"

"Say that again?"

"I don't know what I mean. But I think there's so much room in each of us…You can love more than one person the most. I'm not making sense."

"Making sense never matters," he says.

I lace the fingers of my other hand through the fingers of his other hand, so we're holding both hands. "You have so many amazing songs in you."

"You think so?"

"I know so," I say. "I've seen the future."

He smiles. "Oh! So that's your trick."

"Now you know."

He knows I'm saying goodbye for real this time, but he smiles. The Jimmy Westwood smile. I raise the camera to my eye. Click.

"You know how sculptors say they see the statue in the hunk of marble and carve away everything else?" I say. "You live in the sixties! There are songs everywhere you turn. In all the characters wandering the Haight—in their stories, in their everyday lives. There are songs in the park and in all the things happening in the world—the horrors and the marvels. Like you said, you just have to listen to the city. Not to mention all the songs in your dreams—your sleeping dreams and your daydreams. Jimmy, there are even songs across the bridge. All you have to do is carve away all the nonsense that isn't a song."

We lock eyes.

He picks up the love beads from where they're looped on top of the dress on the bed and lowers them over my head. "Take these with you."

I can't kiss him again. Too wonderful, too painful, too everything.

I close the door behind me. By the time I'm halfway down the stairs I hear the strumming of Jimmy's guitar. He sings a bar, *"More than one only one…"*

"SPEED? ACID? LIDS?" THE corner pusher hits me up. I rush past him in the morning mist. I watch TV. I'm used to ignoring drug ads and their litany of side effects. Maybe this guy should adopt their practice: "Side effects may include paranoia, memory loss, convulsions, sleep disturbances, tremors, irritability, and bad trips. If you have a case of the munchies that lasts longer than four hours, go to your nearest 7-Eleven."

I pass the old Psychedelic Shop. Signs in the window read: "Be Free," "Don't Mourn For Me, Organize" and "Nebraska Needs You More." Huh?

I turn onto Ashbury and pass the Grateful Dead House. Two band members are being led out by some cops and a couple of men in suits with short hair and skinny ties. Narcs.

A guy on the corner hands out a newspaper. He wears a fatigue jacket and a flat-topped hat with a feather. "Our first issue," he says. I take one. It's published by the Free City Collective. The front page informs me that inside I'll find instructions on how to build a firebomb.

I pick up my pace, mentally running through the elements required to get me home: darkroom, camera…darkroom, camera… and a final goodbye to Jimmy, the goodbye that proved I mean business, that demonstrated commitment to my own time. Surely, the universe will take note of that.

I bound up the back steps to Vic's apartment. The door into the kitchen is unlocked, as usual, but Vic isn't there. I hurry through the living room to the darkroom. I close the door, flip on the red light, and pull out my phone. Nothing. I do a quick sweep of the room, searching for something that might be the missing element. Anything. The pictures from my roll of film still hang on the cord across the room, dry now. I pull down two: the one of Jimmy and me and the close-up of my locket. I close my eyes and press the photos against my heart. Eyes closed, I reach for my phone and press the power button. I open my eyes. Nothing. What am I missing?

Tears prick the back of my eyes. I'm stranded.

I hear footsteps climbing the back stairs. I drop the two photos on the counter and dart out of the darkroom through the living room into the kitchen where I throw open the back door. Vic is making his way up the stairs holding a grocery bag in each arm.

The missing thing is Vic?

"Hello! Hello!" he says, not one bit rattled by my appearing from inside his apartment.

"I'm sorry I let myself in," I say.

"You're always welcome." He pauses to catch his breath even though there are only a few steps to go. I grab one of the bags. He takes hold of the railing with his free hand and takes a deep breath.

"You okay?" I ask.

"I'm fine," he says. "Perfectly fine. Not young, but fine."

I help him unpack the groceries.

A lot of canned garbage. "You should be eating healthier," I say. As I pull out a can of Spaghetti-O's, it hits me. I forgot the back stairs. It has to be: darkroom, camera, back stairs.

Darkroom.

"Can I see the pictures?"

He leads me into the darkroom and begins unclipping the photos from the line. He sees the two pictures I'd already pulled off, now lying on the counter. "Those are my favorites, too," he says.

I pick them up, study them for a moment. "You keep them."

"No, no, you should have them. They're your work."

"Not this one," I say. I hand him the cropped shot of my locket. "You did this." I rest my palm on the locket beneath my sweater. "Besides, I've got this."

"Fair enough," he says. He taps the other photo in my hand. It's the selfie of me and Jimmy reflected in the plate glass. "But not this one," he says. "You should have this one." A couple of hippies, arms around each other, grinning in love. I stare at it, flashing on the moment I came upon a picture of my own parents, young and in love, before…before they weren't. Assuming I make it home, will this picture poke at Joni's life? Or mine? Will it lift me or haunt me?

"No," I say. "I want you to have it to remember me by."

"You're going away?" he says.

I nod.

"You can come back any time, you know."

I nod again. Even though I don't know. I don't know if I can and I don't know if I would even if I could. I don't know if I should. But I can live with that.

And why is it harder to say goodbye to Vic than it was to Jimmy? I throw my arms around him and hold him tight. I feel the nub of his ubiquitous gray sweater. He pats my back—there, there. "You okay, honey?"

"I hope so," I say. "I think so."

He steps out of my hug, holds me at arm's length to look at me. "I'm always here, you know," he says.

"I know." I do know that. He'll always be with me. "Because all that really matters is to be there for the people who mean something."

"That's about the size of it," he says. "You must've heard that from someone pretty smart." He winks. It was him, of course.

He gives the Leica hanging around my neck a little pat.

"I'll take good care of it," I say.

"I know you will," he says. "You better skedaddle. I have work to do." He says that because he knows I'm having a hard time leaving (if I *can* leave), not because he wants to get rid of me.

"Goodbye," I say. I feel compelled to say it out loud so the universe or the pluriverse or the multiverse or whatever it is I need on my side doesn't have any wiggle room.

I walk out of the darkroom and close the door behind me. The red light over the door flashes on. As I pass through the living room into the kitchen, I grip the Leica hanging around my neck like the talisman it is. Darkroom. Camera. Back stairs. I open the kitchen door that leads to the rickety staircase as though I were about to hurl myself off a cliff. Then I head down those stairs.

Halfway down I hear a familiar ping. My hand flies to my phone in my back pocket. The screen lights up with Joni's face. Her eyes—sepia-toned—are the same shade as Vic's.

CHAPTER FOURTEEN

It's like landing after a cross-country flight. Emails and texts download one after the other. Nothing says *Welcome Home* like so much spam. But the endless dinging sounds like a jackpot to me.

I land at the bottom of the stairs in front of the Amazon pick-up center, facing a wall of Amazon trucks, smiley arrow after smiley arrow. I head east to where I left my car. There's a Pilates studio and a high-end bicycle store; craft cocktail bars and coffee roasters; a tapas joint and a counterculture museum. That is: a *museum* of the counterculture. I pass the homeless huddled in doorways—castaways, not runaways. I pass a guy walking down the street screaming at no one—not tripping, but on a call.

I pass Amoeba Music. A new text chimes. It's Nathan. Yay!

—*Probably little late. In the city. Dim sum.*

I text back.

—*Where? I'm in city too.*

—*Yank Sing. On Stevenson. Join us!* Smiley face, fingers crossed.

I don't want to steal any of his time with Joni, but I'm desperate to see her, to know she exists as her silly, extraordinary self—that I didn't change her in any way by taking a joyride through time.

—*On my way.*

—*Party Popper emoji.*

Miraculously, there is no parking ticket on the windshield of my car. There's the car seat, right where it belongs. I slide behind the wheel and set the Leica on the passenger seat. My finger feels something wedged in the crease of the seat. I dig it out. It's an errant bead, a flat disc. Lapis lazuli, I think. No, it's more green than blue, must be jasper. I don't remember that one from the strand that broke, never noticed it. It's smooth and cool to the touch, wanting to be rubbed like a worry stone. There's always worry when you're a mom. Vic reminded me of that. But not right this minute… I'm going to be holding Joni soon.

I drive past the row of Victorian houses known as the Painted Ladies. I take a certain pride in their celebrity. We were the first to paint a Victorian house like a Fabergé egg. I drive through Hayes Valley where trendy is having a moment. But not like a sixties moment. Not so compelling that kids are making a pilgrimage from all over the country to breathe the air there. I stop at a red light in the heart of the city center opposite Bill Graham Civic Auditorium. I've never been inside. I should go to a concert there sometime. But there won't be posters covered in liquid lettering or a copper bucket full of apples for the taking. I circumvent the ghost town that is Union Square. It's worth a few extra minutes to avoid seeing the elegant destination department stores in their current state: empty and deserted. So many excursions that thrilled me as a child. I'll have to find other lunchrooms, other tea rooms, for fine lady outings with Joni.

I burst into the dim sum restaurant. There's a line of people waiting to be seated, but I march straight to the host. "My party is already here."

"We don't seat incomplete parties," he says.

"They didn't know they were incomplete when they got seated," I say. "I promise, my people are here." I move my way through the waiting throng before he can respond. I scan the dining room. The décor is sleek and contemporary. Large windows provide great shafts of natural light that reflect off the polished wood furnishings. The servers wear black slacks and crisp white shirts as they push the dim sum carts. They smile as I weave through searching for Nathan and Joni. They are welcoming, attentive, friendly—that's no way to serve Chinese food. Haven't they ever heard of Edsel?

I spot Nathan and Joni at a far table. Nathan and Joni and Caroline. Seeing Joni's face fills me with such joy, I don't even care that the lovely Caroline is there. I bounce over to their table and swoop Joni into my arms.

"I missed you so much," I say.

"I missed you too, Mommy," she says, "but we had so much fun."

"I'm so glad. Tell me everything you did."

She rattles off a long weekendful of activity. A movie, two trips to the park, and three trips for ice cream. Current favorite flavor: yuzu. Nathan beams. So does Caroline. Maybe Jennifer was onto something. The more people who love my child, the better. I'm not delusional. Mommy and Daddy in two different houses is not ideal. But if it is what it is—which it is—then I have to want the other house, the Daddy house, to be full of love, too.

Joni spots a pushcart bearing char sui bao—palm-sized buns, pillowy white like a spongey meringue.

"Puffy buns!" says Joni. Nathan hails the server, holding up two fingers. The server places two plates of buns on our table which is already covered in plates. "Mommy!" Joni says. "I want to be a puffy bun for Halloween!"

"Great idea!" I say. "We'll have to learn how to say 'trick or treat' in Chinese!"

"Caroline speaks Mandarin," says Nathan.

"Just a little," Caroline demurs.

There was a time—like a couple of days ago—when I would have pulled a muscle trying not to say something snarky. At the very least I would have muttered "Of course she does" as in: we're talking about the lovely Caroline; it's only natural that she speaks seven languages and can tie the stem of a maraschino cherry into a knot with her tongue. But I don't pull a muscle. I don't even have the urge to snark.

Instead, I say, "Wow, that's amazing. Do you know how to say 'trick or treat?'"

Caroline laughs. "I don't think so. But I can find out."

I peel the paper off the bottom of a bao and bite through the fluffy bun into the sticky pork filling—a little sweet, a little salty, completely delicious.

"What did you do this weekend, Mommy?" says Joni. She peels the paper off her bao and leaves her seat to sit on my lap.

"Oh my goodness!" I say. "I don't know where to begin. I had tea with the king of England. And I took a riverboat cruise down the Mississippi."

"I can spell Mississippi," says Joni.

"Let's hear it," says her dad.

"M-I-S-S-I-S-S-I-P-P-I."

All three of us clap.

"Oh! You got new ones!" Joni touches the string of beads around my neck.

"I did!"

We hail more dim sum, adding to the stacks of plates. When it's time to go, Nathan kisses Joni goodbye and Caroline gives her a hug. Nathan and I hug too. Caroline and I aren't quite there yet, but I think we might be some day. Or maybe not. Either way, we'll make it work.

Joni and I hold hands as we head to the car. She's practicing her skipping and I have to throw in a skip or two to keep up.

"So," I say, "it sounds like you had a great weekend."

"I did! I get why it's called a long weekend. Today's the extra day of not doing the usual."

"That's exactly right. Sometimes not doing the usual is the best way to spend a day."

"I agree," says Joni.

"It's good to change your schedule now and then."

"But some things never change," she says as we pass a giant candy emporium, one of those places where they give you an empty bag and you fill it up with sticky, gummy, retro sweets.

"Like what?" I ask.

"Like family."

We enter the Wonka world and I hand Joni a bag. "What?" I say.

"Family doesn't change. Never ever."

"Who told you that?"

"You did."

"I did?"

I add a scoopful of Swedish fish to the bag.

"You said even if my grown-ups live in different houses, we'd still be a family. We'll always be a family."

"That's true."

"There will always be three of us," Joni says matter-of-factly. She shovels a scoop of jelly beans into her bag. "I don't like the green ones."

"That's okay, I'll eat those," I promise.

She fills the bag to the top. As I'm paying for our haul, I notice Joni's shoelace is untied and squat to tie it.

"I can do it," says Joni.

I'm eager to get out of here and go home. Actually, it's kind of stunning how much I'm looking forward to cuddling up on the couch with Joni and watching *Inside Out 2* for the umpteenth time. She loves it when Anxiety goes haywire. Probably reminds her of me. Even so, I say, "Okay, give it a try." I watch as she bends down and takes the ends of the lace in her two hands.

"Bunny ear…bunny ear…" she mutters. "Cross over…cross over…pull the ears." She stares at her shoelace tied in a bow, then looks up at me, amazed.

"You did it!" I squeal.

"Easy peasy lemon squeezy!" she says.

"I'm so proud of you."

"I know," she says. "Me too."

We leave with enough candy to keep us both hyper for days. What more could you want?

We're almost to the car when The Spice Girls sing from my phone: "*Mama, my friend...*" (I refuse to be embarrassed by how much I worshipped them when I was seven. There, I've said it.)

"Hi, Mom."

"Just checking in," she says. "We're on our way to that memorial for Bob's old friend. From his band a thousand years ago."

Sucker punch. "That's today?" I ask. I've lost track of time—this present time—like I haven't changed the clocks for cosmic daylight savings. My brain recalibrates, adjusting for major cognitive dissonance, as Nathan would say. I just spent the past three days with a Jimmy who was very much alive.

"Uh-huh, at four," says my mom. "We wondered if you and Joni wanted to meet us for dinner in the city after."

"We're in the city right now."

"Perfect!" I hear her tell Bob, "It just so happens they're in the city." Then back to me, "Where should we go?"

"I don't know. Where's the thing?"

"The memorial? Some old house in the Haight."

"We can just meet you there," I say.

"You don't have to do that."

"No problem."

"That's so nice of you." Again, to Bob, "They're going to stop by the memorial." I can't make out what he says, but she answers him, "They don't mind. And we'll all have dinner after."

She rattles off the address. Weird to hear it out loud.

Joni pulls something out of her jacket pocket. It's the special Christmas candy bead from the broken string. She holds it up to me, grinning. My eyes go wide and my mouth forms a big "O." I say goodbye to my mom and click off the call. I grasp the bead between two fingers. "Our favorite!"

"Maybe we can add this one to your new ones."

"I'm sure we can," I say, tucking it deep in my pocket.

We arrive at the car. I lift her into her car seat. Then I take the beads off my neck and slide them over her head onto hers.

"I can wear them?" she says.

"Absolutely."

"I'll be super super careful."

"I know," I say. "But if these break, we'll keep the ones we can find and get new ones to go with them."

I buckle her into her seat, then slide behind the wheel and pull away from the curb.

CHAPTER FIFTEEN

I DO MY BEST explaining to Joni about a memorial. We haven't had the death conversation in any depth. Thankfully, we haven't had to. All her grandparents are still around, and we rejected the idea of goldfish when she realized you can't take them out of the water to play with them. We spent several days riffing on "fish out of water."

I park a few blocks away. As we walk to the house, I tell her that a friend of Grandpa Boo-Boo's got very, very old, which is beyond weird to say about the very, very young man I just left. I'm careful not to say that he was sick because: a) I know you're not supposed to say that to little kids so they won't think they're going to die every time they get the sniffles, and b) I don't even know if he was sick. I don't know how or why he died. I was so stunned by the fact of his death that I forgot to ask. I tell her that Boo-Boo's friend got so old that his body didn't work anymore. I tell her that this particular friend was a musician and that his music will always remind us of him and in that way he's still alive...sort of. She seems to get it, though she is curious about whether he will be there and she will see his worn-out body. I'm not sure if that fascinates or terrifies her since she seems both disappointed and relieved when I tell her she doesn't have to worry about that.

The old Victorian has been transformed, the exterior paint job subdued. The fuchsia, lime green, and daffodil yellow have been replaced by dove gray and teal. Exuberance given way to sophistication.

Music wafts from the house. A familiar song. My dad used to sing along—off-key—whenever it played on the radio as he drove me home on Sunday nights. I think the song is from the seventies?

Eighties? One of those groups like Kansas…Boston…Chicago? America, maybe? Definitely not Jimmy's voice. Whatever the group, it must be a song that meant something to him, now part of his send-off playlist.

My mother hovers by the door. When she spots Joni and me coming up the front steps, she crouches low and spreads her arms wide to swoop Joni into a grandma hug. "This means a lot to Bob…" she says. "That you came. Like he's really part of the family."

A twinge of FOMO shoots through me when Joni squeezes my mother tight, burrowing into her. As if on cue, Joni looks up at me, releases one arm from around her grandmother and offers it out to me. "Group hug," she says. I fold myself in, one arm around each of them. "Group hugs are the best," Joni says.

Mom looks at me over Joni's head. "You look great, so well rested…" She takes in my outfit. "And so casual."

I look down at my jeans and sweater. A string of excuses occurs to me, but I refrain from spewing them. "I'm a creative," I say, slightly chagrinned to jump on the adjective-as-noun bandwagon.

The three of us wend our way through the crowd. It's a full house. Didn't I just see this house full of people gathered to celebrate Jimmy Westwood and his hit song? It's head-snapping. Of course, these folks are older. They're grown-ups…and then some.

Mom heads for Boo-Boo who talks animatedly with a small group.

A woman in her fifties approaches me. Her salt-and-pepper hair is cut in a serviceable bob. She wears black slacks with a cream-colored tunic.

"Would you like to sign the guest book?" she says, offering me the green leather book in her hand. She flips to a blank page and hands me a pen. "Write as much you like."

I stare at the page, gilt-edged and bordered by a curlicue of vine. My heart jangles as I struggle to find words. Finally, I write: "You changed the world one heart at a time." I sign my name, Tamara.

Not Mari. No last name. Then I close the book and hand it back to her.

"I'm Tommi," she says.

"Mari," I say. "And this is Joni."

Joni extends her little hand. The lady shakes it. "Nice to meet you, Joni."

"I have a friend named Tommy," says Joni. "He's a boy."

Tommi smiles. "A lot of Tommy's are boys. But I have an 'i' at the end of my name instead of a 'y.' It's short for Tomorrow."

Of course it is.

I look hard. I can almost see that baby in there… I *can* see her. It's all I can do not to throw my arms around her.

"I like it," says Joni.

"Thank you," she says. "So do I. Even though it's a funny name. My parents were children of the sixties. Big time."

I nod. They sure were. "I'm sure that's true of a lot of the people here."

She chuckles. A young man and woman slide into our little circle. "This is my son, Ethan, and his wife, Annie," says Tomorrow. Ethan and Annie are a little younger than I am, but not much. We nod hellos.

My mom returns to lead Joni by the hand into the dining room where a few children are playing.

I try to be cool. "I think I might have met your mother once," I say to Tomorrow. "Is she here?"

"She died last year," she says.

Jimmy gone. Jennifer gone. Tomorrow all grown up with a grown-up, married child of her own. It's too much. A calculus too strange to ponder.

"I'm so sorry," I say to Tomorrow. There's so much I want to tell her—how it was Jennifer, her mother, who found me after my bike accident, appearing like a dryad, her hair cascading to her waist; how it was her mother who made me come with them to the city;

how it was her mother who, this second time around, taught me that there can never be too many people to love your child. Instead, I say, "Your mother made the best granola."

"She did!" says Tommi. "Her whole thing started out as broken cookies. Some friend of hers said she should call it granola and people would love it just like that. I was kind of hoping they might be here today so I could say thank-you."

My mind scrambles for a story that makes sense of that friend being me—the friend who was also responsible for Tomorrow being born at The Fillmore. Impossible.

"Is your dad here?"

"He really wanted to be but he's gigging with a band on a cruise ship. I think he's in Santorini right now. Dubrovnik maybe. I lose track."

She smiles and moves on to offer the green leather book to another guest.

I struggle to get my bearings. The parlor where I'm standing is entirely redone. The maroon settee has been replaced by a vanilla sectional; the overstuffed easy chairs by a couple of ultra-low leather slings, the kind that look so hip no one will admit they're fiercely uncomfortable.

I feel like I'm in one of those dreams where you know you're in a certain place, a place you know very well, but everything about it is different.

I navigate the crowd on my own. It's an eclectic group: friends, old hippies from the neighborhood, record exec types. A circle of guests huddles in the corner of the room. Someone is holding court: "There's this explorer flying over the Himalayas, and this big storm comes up and the plane crashes. He's lost for weeks. Living on nothing but snow. He's close to death, crawling along on his hands and knees when, suddenly, his head bumps into something. He looks up and lo and behold, he sees a giant neon sign. Himalaya Restaurant. Specialty of the house…Shlemma Pie."

"P.J.!" I call his name without thinking. The guy pauses the joke and turns his gaze on me. He's too young to be P.J. He rakes his hand through his blond hair.

"Sorry," I say. "I thought you were someone else. I used to know someone who told that joke all the time. Like on repeat."

"Rodriguez?"

"Yeah," I say. "P.J. You know him?"

"Yeah, we were in a band together. The Lower Companions."

"Were?" I say. "Please don't tell me…"

"No, no, no. Nothing like that. He's in rehab. Promises in Malibu." He holds up both hands, two sets of fingers crossed. "Ninth time's the charm, right?"

I flash on P.J.: that brown capsule in the limo; his fidgeting feet at the press conference; his fingers clutching a flour-coated wad of cash.

I nod and wander into the kitchen. Like the parlor, this is not the kitchen I knew. The funk factor has been streamlined into oblivion. Quartz countertops, pendant lighting, stainless steel appliances… except for the antique white enamel range, the heart of the kitchen. They kept that. Some things are irreplaceable.

A middle-aged man in a suit and tie chats with a vintage Haight character wearing a necktie over a tie-dyed T-shirt. "Mark my words," says the Suit, "vinyl will stick around for good this time. Analog produces a much more natural sound, more nuanced, more depth."

The hippie nods, his long gray ponytail thwacking against his back. "I can dig it," he says. "Plus you get to flip the thing over to the other side." He flings his fingertips at his temples—brain explosion.

"Nothing like the feel in the room when you drop a needle on vinyl," says the Suit.

I get it. It's like feeling the click of the shutter when you snap a shot. You can't reproduce that digitally.

I move on to the backyard. It's the kind of radiant San Francisco afternoon that attracts film crews. People gather around a woman nestled in a rattan bucket swing hanging from the giant Sycamore in the corner, from the very same limb that used to support the old wicker double-seater. The woman is in her late seventies, gray hair piled on top of her head and caught into a pounded silver clip, the kind you have to stab with some sort of skewer. She wears a long, flowing purple dress. Well-worn suede boots poke out from under the hem. Everyone streams toward her, kissing her on the cheek and clasping her in prolonged hugs.

Nina—her jaw less sharp, her eyes less fierce, her body less coiled to spring. But still Nina.

I piece together that Jimmy and Nina were married for over fifty years. That puts their getting married not all that long after my time with them, maybe three or four years. Sounds about right. That's how long it must have taken for Nina to stop pretending she was so tough and for Jimmy to realize there didn't have to be just one The One. Even though, let's face it, Nina was always going to be his one.

There's a break in the river of people flowing past Nina. I work up the nerve to approach her. She looks up at me from the swing. "Hello."

"Hello," I say. "I'm so sorry for your loss."

She studies my face. "Remind me of how we know each other."

"I'm here with Bob and Diana. Boo-Boo, I mean." I say. "I'm Diana's daughter."

"Thank you for coming."

I'm sure she's not one bit interested in talking to me, but she has the learned good grace not to look beyond me, not to do that cocktail party thing when people scan over your shoulder for someone with better chit-chat cache.

"I'm a fan," I say. "You're so talented." I never told her that. It was easier to be the opposite point on that triangle if I didn't admit how talented she was. From this perspective, the triangle was always skewed in her favor, both for the obvious reason (that they lived at the same time) and because there was undeniable musical magic between her and Jimmy.

"Thank you," she says. She sets the swing swaying slightly back and forth. "I was. A long, long time ago," she says matter-of-factly. "Did you have a favorite song?" She's not fishing. It's more like she wants to be reminded.

"I guess…"

"It's okay," she laughs "You can say it. 'Tamara Moonlight.' There's nothing wrong with having that as your favorite. It's everyone's favorite. And it's not like we had very many."

"Was it Jimmy's favorite?" I ask before I can stop myself.

She looks at me strangely. "Why do you ask?"

"Oh, I don't know. I'm interested in how people approach their creative pursuits and what sort of long term legacy their work leaves, not only with their audience, but with themselves…forgive the redundancy…legacy implies long term, doesn't it…?" She looks at me even more strangely. I squeal to a stop, stomping on the verbal brakes a little too late.

"He always made fun of me for being jealous of that song, but…" Her eyes fill with tears. One rolls down her cheek, then another. She doesn't bother to wipe them away. There will just be more.

"I'm sorry," I say. "I didn't mean to…"

She waves away my apology. "You remind me so much of someone," she says. "I don't know who."

"I hate it when that happens. But you know what they say. Everyone has a doppelganger."

"It's not just how you look. It's…more than that," she says. "What did you say your name was?"

"Mari." There. I said it.

"I knew a Mari once," she says. Sweat gathers at the back of my neck. "At least my son did. He had a girlfriend named Mari for a year or two, but I never met her." She gives me a bit of a side-eye.

"It's an unusual name," I say, borrowing from Tommi with an "i".

She nods, trying to make sense of me, a task I wouldn't wish on anyone. Usually, the next question is: Is it short for something? I can't wait around for that one. Impulsively, I lean down into the cocoon of the swing and give her a hug. She hugs me back.

When we part, she smiles at me. "It will mean so much to James that you came," she whispers. "Between you and me, I think you might be the one that got away."

My face flushes. "Really?"

She raises her index finger to her lips: shhh. "Between you and me," she says again.

I'm so relieved that she thinks I'm that Mari (James's Mari) as opposed to this Mari (Jimmy's Mari)…let alone the truth…which is that I'm both those Maris. Even for me, it's a little too *Chinatown*. "She's my sister *and* my daughter."

I knew that James had an older sibling, but I never met him… just like I never met his parents. I kept his theoretical. The way I made him keep mine. Maybe that's why he lost patience with me. That, and my frantic desire to make a certain kind of life come true, a life that could only include one artist—*moi*—and therefore required a grown-up, preferably with a corner office, for counterbalance and financial security. Joke's on me. That vision backfired in more than enough ways to keep me up nights negotiating for a do-over, in too many ways to count.

I weave through the crowd back inside toward the dining room to check on Joni. As I step into the kitchen, one elderly man instructs another: "No, don't throw that there. That can go in the recyclables." He takes the wine cork from the other guest. "Compostable actually." I mentally rewind his face by several decades. It's Bodhi—stache now pure white, gold stud in his ear.

I stop, within earshot, to pour some juice for Joni. An old, familiar song plays softly from the speaker built into the ceiling.

"Jimmy Westwood was one of the good guys," says Bodhi.

"How long did you know him?" asks another guest.

"We go way back," Bodhi reflects. "I remember the night he wrote this song." He gestures toward the speaker.

"He wrote 'Echoes of the Earth?'" I blurt. Everyone knows that song. It's a veritable anthem. They sing it at Joni's pre-school on Earth Day.

"Yeah," says Bodhi. "A bunch of us were sitting around in this house, as a matter of fact, firing each other up about saving the planet…back when we thought we could…" It's hard to tell if he's making a joke or deadly, existentially serious. "And Jimmy goes into the other room…the dining room, I think… He comes out no more than fifteen minutes later with this song. In its entirety. He played it for us and we were blown away. Absolutely blown away. He said—I'll never forget this—he said the song was just there and all he had to do was carve away the stuff that didn't belong."

"He said that?" I say.

Bodhi nods. He snaps out of his reverie to introduce himself. "Bodhi Reeves."

"I'm Mari." I raise the red Solo cup of juice in greeting.

"How did you know Jimmy?" he asks.

"Long story. Basically, my mother's husband was in Neon Dream. Bob. Boo-Boo."

"Oh wow," says Bodhi. "Family connection."

I smile. "What do you do?" I ask.

"I'm an environmental attorney."

He did it! "Awesome."

He cocks his head, eyes wide. "Lawyers don't usually get that reaction."

I smile. "Changing the law of the land, I hope. At least some of them."

"Uphill battle."

"But worth it," I say. I raise the Solo cup, "I've got a little girl around here somewhere who needs juice,"

"Nice meeting you," he says, "though I kind of feel like…"

I interrupt him before he can finish the thought. "Nice meeting you, too."

I pass through the parlor. One of the suit guys peruses the framed photos that line the mantle and cluster on every table. He pauses in front of a picture of Neon Dream—all five of them: Jimmy, P.J., Boo-Boo, Sam, and Nina standing in front of the painted VW van. In that summer of '67, I was the one who gathered the band in front of the van. I was the one who took that picture. It was the picture that became the cover of their one and only album as well as the cover of their hit single, "Tamara Moonlight."

The Suit picks up the photograph in its chunky wooden frame. "Now that's a shot," he says. "They don't make album covers like that anymore."

"Do they make album covers at all?" I ask.

"They do, but most people only see them as thumbnails on their phone. Or if Fallon holds it up before introducing the band."

"Too bad," I say.

"I think that's going to change with vinyl getting so big again." (Oh yeah, he was the guy hyping vinyl earlier.) "There aren't a lot of photographers who can do this anymore," he says as he taps the glass. "I wonder if this guy is still around," he muses.

Inside, I'm that kid in class with my arm stretched high waving my hand wildly in the air. "Pick me, pick me!" Outside, a modicum of cool prevails. "I'm a photographer." I've never said that out loud before, certainly not to a stranger.

"Really?"

"Yes."

"Would I have seen any of your work?"

"Not unless you've been house-hunting in the North Bay."

He tilts his head and squints.

I was all about convincing Jimmy to believe in himself, but now I realize how much Jimmy believed in me. Beneath layers of sarcasm and snark, of condescension and mockery...pushing aside all the psychic contortions I perform to protect myself...from that deep place, I say, "I could take a picture like that. I promise you."

He looks at me for a beat, then reaches into his breast pocket, pulls out a business card, and hands it to me. "Call me about that," he says. "I mean it."

I shove the card into the pocket of my jeans. (Jeans. They're okay. I'm a creative...type.)

"Jordan Tucker," he says, extending his hand. "Do you have a manager?"

We shake. "I do not."

"Nina could probably hook you up," he says.

"Nina?"

"I don't think her company reps photographers, just composers and songwriters, but I'm sure she must know people. Or know people who know people."

"Good to know," I say. Wow. Nina segued to the business side. Makes perfect sense. Her gifts were twofold: that powerful, soul-stirring voice and her hell-bent, single-vision drive.

I excuse myself to look for Joni. I pass through the foyer and glance up the stairs. The giant yin-yang tapestry that hung in the stairwell has been replaced by a series of gold records...and platinum, too...all in identical silver frames. I climb the first few stairs to read the labels on the records. Some of the song titles are familiar, some not. Same with the artists. Not my era. Well, one of them might be from my quasi-era, the late sixties. The plaques mounted under the shiny records behind the glass are all engraved with the same acknowledgment: "Presented to Jimmy Westwood in recognition of your outstanding songwriting contributions..." One after the other. Jimmy Westwood...Jimmy Westwood...Jimmy Westwood.

I freeze there on the landing to study the records commemorating Platinum Sales, Gold Sales, Gold Sales. I breathe in this new reality—Jimmy wrote these songs. And how many more?

Neon Dream may have been a one-hit wonder, but Jimmy Westwood had a big, sparkly career after all. Maybe because I encouraged him. Maybe I had nothing to do with it. I'll never know. But I'll smile every time I hear any one of his songs, no matter who's singing.

More of the collection of golds and platinums continues along the hallway upstairs, but I don't go up. I don't want to be tempted to peek into Jimmy's old room. I'll keep the version of that room in my mind's eye…and my camera's.

I find Joni in the dining room. A buffet is laid out, but Joni and a few other kids have staked out a corner of the floor, a world of Calico Critters spread out before them. I had no idea they still made the Critters—the rabbits, bears, mice, and the rest—which I remember from my own childhood.

Another familiar song drifts from the speaker in this room. Now I get it. This is not a playlist of Jimmy's favorites. It's a playlist of songs Jimmy wrote.

Joni picks up a Calico cat and runs her finger across the fuzzy flocking. She looks up at me, "Hi, Mommy, this is Catty."

"Hello, Catty," I say.

"She's going to the fair with her friends."

"Sounds like fun."

Joni toddles the tiny figure along the floor, then turns to a little girl about nine years old. "This is my friend, Luna."

"Hi, Luna."

Luna has honey brown hair tied in a purple velvet ribbon at the top of her head. Her eyes are the color of the bottom of the ocean, dark gray-green flecked with gold. The first and only other time I saw eyes that color was when I climbed into a VW van the morning after my bike accident and looked into the eyes of the guy behind the wheel. Jimmy's eyes.

I kneel on the floor next to them and pick up a Calico bear. "Can I come to the fair?" I growl.

"Sure!" says Joni.

"Sure!" says Luna. She looks up from the elaborate village of critters. "Hi, Uncle James!"

I look up.

"Mari!" It's James. My James. He's rocking a three-day stubble that's flecked with gray, morphing him from the cute boy I remember to dashing man. As in: hot.

"What are you doing here?" he wonders.

"We came with my mom and Bob…her husband…Bob…Bob was in the band with your dad." My heart stumbles a few beats. I knew how seeing him would feel. I just didn't know how much it would feel.

"Oh," he says. There's a lot to the way he says that single word, like maybe that wasn't the reason he was hoping for. Maybe he was hoping I'd come for him. Or I could be hoping he was hoping. But I do glimpse him glancing at my ringless ring finger.

"Do you want to play, Uncle James?" Luna asks.

Of course. Those eyes. Luna is Jimmy's grandchild. To me, he may have been frozen in time—the way you think of other people's children never getting older even as you watch your own child grow and age—but in the fullness of his life Jimmy was a father and a grandfather.

"You can be a hedgehog," Luna continues.

"Sure, Lulu" he says. He folds his long legs to sit cross-legged on the floor with us.

"Criss-cross applesauce," says Joni.

"Their heads turn," says Luna, swiveling a hedgehog head as she hands it to James. He takes it. No wedding ring.

"What are you doing these days?" James asks without looking up from the critter village.

"Aside from...." I gesture toward Joni. "This is Joni."

"Hi, Joni," he says.

"Hi," says Joni, wobbling her little critter back and forth as though it were doing the talking.

"I'm still taking pictures," I say.

"That's great."

"Pictures of staged houses for real estate agents."

"Nothing wrong with that," he says.

I shrug. "How about you?"

"Still writing music. Mostly commercials. But I've scored a couple of movies."

"That's amazing! Your dad would be so proud of you," I say. "I mean, I'm sure he was. Of course he was. I'm so sorry, by the way. I can't believe I didn't say that already. I'm so sorry for your loss. It must be…I can't even…"

"It's weird," he says. "At least for the moment, that's as far as I can go. How weird it is that he's not here anymore. That, like, his time was up." His eyes land on the love beads hanging around Joni's neck. "All we have is this moment and then you string them all together and that's a life… He got to the last bead on the string… and poof?" He unfolds his long legs and stands.

I place my Calico bear on the porch of the mini log house. I stand and wrap my arms around James and hold him. He holds me, too, and we stay like that, in each other's arms for longer than a condolence hug requires.

"I always picture you taking pictures," he says into my hair, my head against his chest.

"Remember the picture I took of you the day we met?"

"I do."

"It won a prize?"

"I remember."

"It's one of my favorite pictures I ever took."

We release each other and put just enough air between us so we can lock eyes.

"Truth," I say. "But I'm going to start again. Shooting people, not just houses."

"You should."

Joni bounces up from the floor. She thrusts her arm in front of my face. "Look, Mommy! Luna gave me this." She snaps a stretchy beaded bracelet on her wrist.

"That was so nice of her."

"She got to see Taylor Swift," says Joni. "Everyone trades bracelets there."

"So I've heard," I say.

"Uncle James took me," Luna adds.

"Wow" I say. "That's…just wow!"

Joni has the situation wired. "I'll have to give her something next time we have a playdate because I can't give her this…" She fingers the strand of love beads around her neck. "Right?" She gives me the look that means: help me out here.

"Right. You can't give her those. Those are very special to both of us." I turn to Luna. "You understand, right, Luna?"

"Sure," she says, unphased. "I get it."

"She gets it," echoes James.

A man appears in the doorway. Bald with a gray fringe and a hefty gut, half-hidden by an unbuttoned vest hanging over nondescript gray trousers. He pushes his glasses up on his nose as he beckons James. "Your mom's looking for you." That inimitable rasp—a voice more gravelly with age but that could only belong to Royce.

"Got it," James says, heading out. Then to me, "Thanks for coming." He smiles.

So do I.

Royce stands there, unmoving. "Friend of James's?"

"Yes," I say. "And Bob's. Boo-Boo's."

He adjusts his hearing aid deeper into his ear. "Oh yeah?"

"He's married to my mom… I've heard a lot of stories." I twirl a finger in the air around me. These walls *did* talk.

A sly smile sneaks across his face. "I bet," he says. "I managed the band for a minute-and-a-half… When they had their big hit."

He might be waiting for me to respond. I don't.

"'Tamara Moonlight'" he prompts. "You know it?"

"I do."

"Great times." He shakes his head, calculating how long those times have been gone. "The best times…"

"I'm sorry…" I say, "for your loss…" I study his face—puffy, yet deflated. There's a lifetime of bluster there. I thought he'd probably hit some kind of stride when the greed-is-good era rolled around, but no. Even at this advanced age, he's got the expression of a man still looking to make it, hungry for attention unearned. "The loss of your friend, I mean," I say. But Royce's loss is bigger than Jimmy. His real loss is the thing he never had.

Even so, I have a hard time mustering sympathy.

The sharp clink of a knife against glass calls everyone to the foyer and the parlor. The music stops. It's speech time.

Boo-Boo steps to the microphone set up at the foot of the stairs. "Even though I've moved to Nob Hill and gone all bougie, a piece of my heart has always stayed in this house. Today, man, they've really taken another little piece of my heart… See what I did there?" Groans. He tells a few stories of back in the day and everyone laughs when he finishes because Joni applauds like absolute crazy.

I had to make a surreal trip—a veritable trip-and-a-half—to learn what Joni already knows about grandfathers. I have never been, nor will I ever be, one of those people who keeps a gratitude journal, but I must admit that when I think about my bizarre and tortuous journey to discovering my grandfather Vic, I am so filled with gratitude that it's nearly impossible to contain. I think of the little ditty my father sang to me when I was small: "*I love you so much / I can't conceal it / I love you so much / It's a wonder you don't feel it!*" Now that I know Vic, it seems like the kind of thing he would have sung to my dad when he was a little boy. A legacy of photographs and silly songs. It could be worse.

An old woman (my mother would call her "older") in an expensive suit (Chanel, maybe?) turns out to be Jimmy's sister. She tells us about his childhood and college days, about how distraught their parents were when he dropped out of school to pursue his music. That's what she says: "his music" in the way their parents must have spat out the phrase. She throws in something about his having shown "so much promise in the sciences" whatever that means. It's a weird speech for a memorial, but what do I know about memorial speeches. All I know is, she may have grown up in the same house with him, but she never knew the boy who raced to the record store with two weeks' worth of allowance in his pocket.

Next, Royce crosses to the mic, the shadow of a swagger bleeding through. "I'm Royce," he says. "Jimmy and I go way back. I managed Neon Dream…Jimmy…," he drifts. There's too much history there to express. "I can do this," he says, his voice cracking, which is so bizarre because Royce's whole gestalt was being the coolest guy in the place, a guy who would never let them see you sweat, let alone cry.

He casts his eyes upward for inspiration. "Let me just say, we understood each other, me and Jimmy. Over the years, he used to write to me. As good as he was with lyrics, he wrote even better letters. No matter where I lived, the letters came. Real letters about the good old days and all the crazy times we had. Then emails. And then after I was away for a little while there, you dig…"

A guy standing behind me whispers to someone next to him, "Nineteen months for crypto fraud."

"He started a music trivia group text," Royce continues, "with a posse that's getting smaller all the time…They were fewer and farther between in the last few years when…you know, he was getting weaker…" He shakes his head again. "But he kept those messages coming when he could. I was the guy with the connections, but Jimmy…he was all about connection. One on one."

So that was it. Jimmy was sick. For years, at least a few. It's impossible to conjure him diminished, as anything other than his young self, robust and animated, energized with possibility. Easier to think of him going out in a flash. My face must give me away. The woman standing next to me, an earth mother type with a hefty crystal pendant nestling between her bosoms, rests a hand on my shoulder to comfort me. I shake my head, both in disbelief and to scatter loose the mental pixels before they coalesce into an image of Jimmy less than.

Royce hands the mic to Nina and edges himself back into the crowd. He squeezes in next to a statuesque redhead in a leather pencil skirt. "Hello, Sunshine." But the glint is gone. He's just another dime-a-dozen leach working as many side hustles as he can. No longer a legend in his own mind.

I gather up Joni and perch her on my hip.

Nina, at the mic, takes a long, deep breath. Then she launches into the story of the night Neon Dream won the Battle of the Bands at The Fillmore. How Jimmy and she had been on a silly "break" from each other at the time.

"We didn't call it that then. Only years later when we were watching an episode of *Friends* did we look at each other and burst out laughing. 'There's a name for that! We were on a break!'" Scattered titters. (The strangest part to me is the notion of Jimmy and Nina watching a sitcom. Even stranger than me being the person who filled that break.) That night, she explains, somebody dragged her from her waitressing shift at a restaurant in Sausalito to drive her to The Fillmore and push her up on stage with the band. She can't remember the name of the restaurant. I can: the Trident. It's all I can do to stop from calling it out.

"It was that night. I remember the moment I found myself on stage across a mic from Jimmy and knew our life was about to change. That was it. It was going to be our life—not mine, not his—but ours."

Her voice catches. She closes her eyes and you can see right through her eyelids that she's traveling back in time. She doesn't have to triangulate her journey with amulets and transports and the red light outside a darkroom door. She simply plumbs her heart and she's there. You can see her make the trip.

"I'm so lucky we had that moment…" she concludes.

She passes the mic to James.

"Dad…" He breathes. "Dad would be horrified if I said he taught me everything I know. He didn't, so he doesn't have to worry about that. But he taught me a lot. What he taught me was to learn everything I could from wherever and whoever I could. He taught me that a life spent making music is something to be proud of. And when one dream doesn't work out, it's okay because you can have more than one. Maybe that's the dream that was meant for you all along. He taught me that music is a force for good. That music is the ultimate time machine."

I'm afraid he's going to look right at me, so I look away. Not that he knows about my weekend getaways to the Summer of Love, but just in case.

"You know what I mean," he goes on. "I hear Nelly doing 'Hot in Herre' and I'm a senior in high school driving Carrie Keller home after seeing *My Big Fat Greek Wedding* which would have been her choice or *Minority Report* which would have been mine. And see…that's the point…I can't remember which movie we saw, but I remember that song came on the radio…that funky beat…infectious…" James bobs his head to the beat in his memory. He can't help himself, starts rapping. *"I was like, good gracious ass bodacious / Flirtatious, tryin' to show face…"*

Everyone laughs. There's James Westwood, troubadour tradition coursing through his veins, rapping his heart out.

"That's just one of my gazillion memories associated with a song. You have them, too. We all do." He scans the crowd gathered in the parlor and spilling beyond. Boomers. "I don't know… What are yours?… You hear… What? You hear 'Sgt. Pepper' and you're walking down Haight heading to the park for…"

"A gathering of the tribes!" Boo-Boo volunteers from the back of the room.

"A gathering of the tribes," James echoes. "My dad used to tell me there was a week when 'Sgt. Pepper' floated out of every window you passed. But the music is more than just what was happening at the time. It's who you were. You time travel to a different version of yourself. Music reminds you of who you were and maybe who you always have been and always will be no matter what."

He inhales. "That's what he taught me. The music remembers."

Applause swells. A man in the back lets loose with, "You're fuckin' right the music remembers. And it's a good thing, 'cause God knows I don't remember shit anymore."

Everyone laughs. A woman wearing dangly shell earrings seconds that, "You said it, Frizz." She twirls the ends of the long gray braid draped over one shoulder.

James extends the microphone. "Anyone else?"

I want to say something. But I can't of course. How would I explain who I am? What story could I tell? The one about how Jimmy picked me up and sang me across the bridge? About how he was my first kiss? About how he encouraged me to take the pictures I wanted to take, not the ones for school credit? How he convinced me that the world was worth changing, that changing it one heart at a time could accomplish that? The story about how he changed my life?

James hands the mic to his older brother who raises his glass. "To Dad. To Jimmy!"

"To Jimmy!"

"To Jimmy!"

"Long may his freak flag fly!" says Boo-Boo. He makes a funny, googly-eyed face at Joni.

James steps to the record player on the credenza under the window. "This was my dad's favorite of his songs," he announces. The room falls quiet as he lifts the needle and drops it onto the vinyl. There is absolute silence except for little pops and clicks as the needle settles into the grooves. And the non-sound behind those little noises—the sound of atmosphere. I await the opening riff of "Tamara Moonlight." But when the music starts, it's something else.

It sounds familiar, but not polished, like when they play early versions of Beatles songs and there's something so startlingly pure about them that it's like you never heard the song before. I close my eyes to listen more closely.

Jimmy's voice is soft and gentle, but certain. *"You tried to escape / But you were always you / You pretended not to / But you knew it was true / Across the noise / Beyond the pain / In the sunlight of hope / And the heartbreak of rain / To every lost forgotten friend / This letter carries hope, hope without end."*

It's the song he was struggling to piece together. "Ten half songs are useless to me," Royce badgered him. This must be the final version of the demo he laid down on the reel-to-reel that day, or some other day. But he did it. He wrote a letter to the world.

Everyone is crying by the end of the song. Including me. Joni takes my hand. "It's okay, Mommy."

James slings an arm around Nina. So does Philip, Luna's dad, standing on her other side. She wraps one arm around one son's waist, buries her head against the other's chest.

People say their goodbyes, kissing Nina one more time, and heading out. My mom finds me. "Shall we?" she says. She hails Boo-Boo who makes his way over.

We wend our way through the crowd. Jimmy got a packed house. And I got to hold onto the people I love the most all in one place.

I spot James and catch his eye just before his buddies surround him. I offer a little wave. He waves back.

On our way out, my mom scans the place. "Do you think she'll want to sell?"

I shoot her a look.

"The house does have great bones," says Joni.

"That's my girl," says Mom.

Mom and Boo-Boo treat Joni and me to a special occasion dinner at the Fairmont's Tonga Room. I haven't been there since I was a little girl, but I still remember the simulated rainstorm and the lagoon in the middle of the room under the straw-covered ceiling and how, from out of nowhere, a band floated out onto the lagoon on a thatch-covered barge. I was gobsmacked. Now it's Joni's turn.

We order pu-pu platter after pu-pu platter. When they bring Joni her virgin pina colada, she secrets the tiny umbrella away in her pocket.

By the time we leave, Joni is logy with coconut shrimp and spareribs and the wonder of a hurricane that blows in and out like magic. Boo-Boo swoops her up in his arms and carries her down the hall into the lobby of the hotel.

She oohs and aahs at the magnificence: columns that support an intricate ceiling, detailed plasterwork, high gloss everything. I excuse myself to look for a ladies' room, but, in truth, I want to have a peek at the Vanderbilt Room. I follow the corridor to the ballroom where the band held their press conference. Then I stop. I don't need to see it. It doesn't matter if the version I remember is real or not. I turn around and head back to the lobby…where Joni practices her skipping on the sparkling marble floor.

Later, in the car heading over the bridge back home, my headlights point the way as Joni and I sing along with the radio like lunatics. "Hot dog, hot dog, hot diggity dog…!"

The song ends and Joni pipes up from her car seat.

"Mommy…" I turn down the radio. "What does my name mean?"

"Your name?"

"Yeah. Joni."

"Well, I don't actually know what your name itself means. We can look that up. But you were named for a wonderful songwriter. Grandma Di-Di's favorite. She wrote the song I used to sing to you every night when you were little."

"The one about the noodles?"

"Noodles?"

"Angel hair."

I laugh. "Noodles are a different kind of angel hair. The song is about angel's hair."

"And clouds."

"And clouds," I say.

Joni sings, *"From up and down and still somehow…"*

"You remember."

"I remember all the songs."

"I'm so glad," I say.

"You were named for a song, too," she says. "Grandma Di-Di told me."

"I was."

"'Tamara Moonlight.' It was Grandma Di-Di's special song with Grandpa. Not Grandpa Boo-Boo, but Grandpa Grandpa."

"That's right."

"Luna's name means moon. She told me. Moon like your name song was about the moon."

"How about that?" I say.

We drive in silence for a few miles. Then, "Mommy?"

"Yes, lovie?"

"Do you know what they call a bunch of ladybugs?"

"I don't think I do."

"A loveliness," she says. "A loveliness of ladybugs!"

"That's lovely," I say.

I think Joni is asleep, but when we're almost home she says, "Mommy, tell me the story."

"Once upon a time," I begin, "there was a summer."

"Is it summer now?" asks Joni.

"Not anymore."

"I like summer best," she says.

"How come?"

"Because you don't have to wear socks."

"That's a good reason. But the other seasons are fun, too."

"What's this one called again?"

"Fall," I say. "Or autumn. Some people call it autumn."

"What's good about autumn?" she wonders, trying on the word.

"Well, for one thing, there's Halloween."

She thinks about that for a while. "Mommy," she says, "I don't want to be a Chinese puffy bun for Halloween anymore."

"Okay." I glance into the rearview mirror. Her eyes are wide with inspiration. "I want to be a hippie."

"I love it!" I say. "You are my little hippie."

"I'll take that as a compliment," she says.

"It is," I say.

"Go on… When you walked down the street, everyone had on bright colors…" she prods.

"And Princess Joni was twirling down the street with a beautiful crown on her head."

"Made of flowers."

"Yes, made of flowers. And she heard a flute playing."

"You mean a recorder."

"Yes," I say, "a recorder."

"And a tambourine…"

"And bells…"

"Tinkling bells…" she says, laughing.

"And the music drifted down the street, getting softer and softer as it got farther and farther away. It was the sound of the circus leaving town."

EPILOGUE

I look down at her brand-new tiny face. Her skin is translucent. Her rosebud mouth opens and closes as she sleeps. Between her golden eyebrows, there's a flat, pink birthmark the size of a dime. The nurse calls it an angel's kiss. She tells me it will disappear within the year, but I'm in no hurry. She has all the time in the world to grow up. Her sister just turned seven. Time rushes by entirely too fast on its own without wishing it away.

A nurse's aide pads in carrying a cluster of pink mini roses stuffed, Martha Stewart style, into a glass cube. She sets the arrangement on the bedside table and hands me the card. "*Welcome to the world! Love, Uncle Nathan and Aunt Caroline.*" A little bubble of snark rises in me. It turns out that snark dies hard, like it's kind of presumptuous of them to assign themselves titles, right? I gaze at the baby in my arms and tamp down my inner cynic. Nathan will be Daddy to one of my daughters and Uncle to the other. Not anything I ever would have imagined, let alone strived for, but I can live with that.

The instant my mother arrives she wants to know, "Who are the flowers from?" When I tell her, she bobs her head from side to side, considering a response. I pre-empt her. "It's super nice of them."

I know she's thinking something derogatory about Nathan. Before Nathan and I split, my mother thought he was "one of the good ones." Not so much anymore. She opens her mouth to speak, but I cut her off again. "Mom, he's still one of the good ones. He just wasn't meant to be my good one."

"When did you get to be so zen?"

"I don't know," I say. "In 1967?"

She laughs at our in-joke. Ever since I found her tattered old scrapbook, with the pictures of her and Dad looking like sixties flower children, I've summoned 1967 as the answer to so many conundrums. It's crazy how often it makes sense, like it marked the beginning of something, or the end of something, or the epitome of something else.

Boo-Boo arrives a few minutes later clutching an oversized plush panda bear. "It called to me from the gift shop," he says.

"You're a crazy person," says my mom.

The baby half-wakes for an instant, then flutters back to sleep. The three of us watch her in silence, sharing the wonder of every millimeter of her exquisite self—the way her hands poke out from the swaddle and tuck under her chin, the dove coo of her breathing, the flicker of a dream across her face.

James pushes open the door, grinning. It's a great grin. The best. Runner-up to no one's. My husband's grin. He leans down to kiss me.

"I love you," I whisper.

"I know," he says. "You love me so much."

When he stands, he's still smiling—at our baby in my arms, at me. Once upon a time, I searched for his father's smile in his, but no more. Turns out Jimmy's smile was meant to show me the way to James's. A portal, I've sometimes thought, to the real magic, the thrumming heartbeat of the here and now.

Joni bursts in behind him with an armload of gifts.

"Oh my goodness!" I say. "What have you got?"

"Presents for the baby!" She bounces from foot to foot. Everyone else arrived last night within the hour after her birth, but Joni was at home with Nathan. "Can I see her?"

"Come sit here on the bed and you can hold her."

Joni positions herself gingerly next to me. James wedges a pillow on her lap and I place the baby in her careful arms. She beams down at her sister. "She's so little."

"That's the way they come," says James. He looks showered and fresh, his gray ocean eyes no longer bleary with nineteen hours of labor. Mine, not his, but tell him that. He kisses me again—on the temple—then perches on the edge of the bed. He rests his hand on the covers over my leg.

"Should we open her presents?" I say.

Joni nods, but she can't take her eyes off her sister in her arms. "She's going to be my best friend," she says.

"She is," I say.

The first gift is a small stuffed panda. The grown-ups laugh. "Great minds think alike," says Boo-Boo.

"What does that mean?" Joni wonders.

"We both had the same great idea because we both have great big minds," he says.

The second present is a framed photograph of Joni. I took this picture about a year ago. She'd come with me to a photo shoot for a band featured in a movie that James had scored. They weren't big—not yet anyway—but they wanted a cool photo for the cover of their demo, so James suggested they hire me. "Hired" is a euphemism since they only paid me in free lunch and tickets to their next show. I snapped this shot of Joni when she was watching the band set up. Six years old and thrilled to be playing with the big kids.

"I love this picture," I say.

"It's for the baby," says Joni. "For her to keep next to her crib so she sees me first thing when she wakes up and last thing before she goes to sleep."

"That's the best idea ever," I say.

"Open the purple one," says Joni.

I unwrap the third gift, heavier than the others.

"I helped wrap it," boasts Joni.

James nods, proud for them both.

The wrapping paper is lavender, covered in cottontails and daisies. I unwrap it slowly; the paper will go in the baby's scrapbook.

I pull out the object inside with great care. Its base is shaped like puffy clouds. A rainbow arcs over the top.

"It's a music box!" squeals Joni.

"Wow!" I say. "She's going to love that."

"Play it, Mommy."

I locate the wind-up key beneath one of the clouds and twist. It takes a few tinkling, metallic notes before I identify the tune. *Somewhere Over the Rainbow…way up high; there's a land that I heard of…* I once climbed into a van driven by a guy gathering his band to head into the city to start their future. As he drove, he tapped the prism dangling from the rearview mirror. It cast rainbows everywhere. He sang, "*Somewhere over the rainbow…way up high…*" I pretended not to, but I couldn't stop watching the rainbows play across his face… Now a memory as ethereal as a rainbow.

"It's the prettiest music box I've ever seen," I say.

"James says babies like music," says Joni.

"They do," I say.

When the song ends, I wind it again. And then once more. Joni raises the baby back to my arms. The baby opens her eyes and takes what I swear is a really good look around, like she's trying to decide if this is the world she pictured.

Joni touches the baby's fingers. "Have we decided yet?" she says. "What her name is?"

"I think we have," I say. I look to James to be sure. He nods.

I kiss the baby between her eyebrows on the spot an angel got to first. "Summer," I say. "Her name is Summer."

ACKNOWLEDGMENTS

Enormous thanks to the usual suspects. I am beyond grateful to them all.

Marianne Moloney whose commitment and enthusiasm are unflagging.

Tyson Cornell for providing me a home at Rare Bird.

Hailie Johnson, my editor at Rare Bird, for asking important questions.

Blair Richwood, an expert and gifted one-person writer's group, whose gravitational force kept this story—and me—from spiraling into time travel chaos.

Profound and inexpressible gratitude for the music that is the heartbeat of this book.